The Kingdoms &

The Elves Of The Reaches

Book II

Robert Stanek

A Keeper Martin's Tale

The Kingdoms & The Elves Of The Reaches Book II

Copyright © 2002 by Robert Stanek.

First Edition, October 2002

Reagent Press

Published by Virtual Press, Inc.

Cover design & illustration by Robert Stanek

ISBN 1-57545-060-7

Reagent Press Books by Robert Stanek

Ruin Mist Tales

The Elf Queen & The King Book 1
The Elf Queen & The King Book 2
The Elf Queen & The King Book 3

Keeper Martin's Tales

The Kindoms & The Elves Of The Reaches, Book 1
The Kindoms & The Elves Of The Reaches, Book 2
The Kindoms & The Elves Of The Reaches, Book 3

Magic Lands: Journey Beyond the Beyond
Ruin Mist Heroes, Legends & Beyond
Magic Lands & Other Stories

Table of Contents

Praise for Ruin Mist &

Keeper Martin's Tale

"A gem waiting to be unearthed by millions of fans of fantasy!"

"Brilliant... an absolutely superior tale of fantasy for all tastes!"

"It's a creative, provoking, and above all, thoughtful story!"

"It's a wonderful metaphor for the dark (and light) odyssey of the mind."

"The fantasy world you have created is truly wonderful and rich. Your characters seem real and full of life."

The Reaches

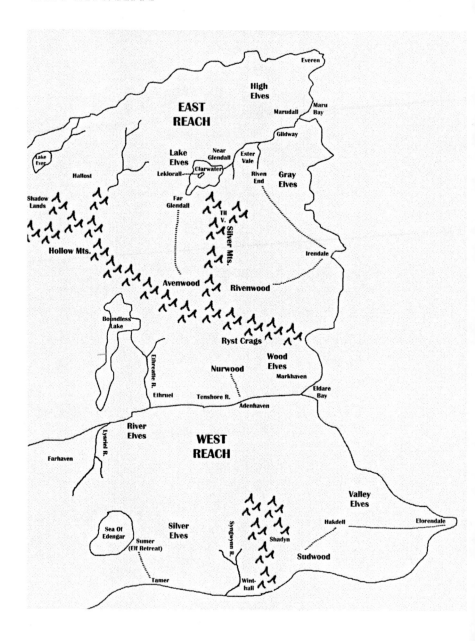

Great Kingdom

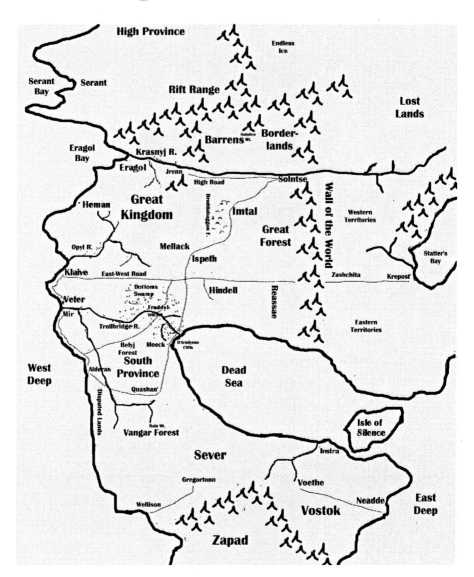

Where The Tale

Ended Last Time

"Father Jacob, will she be all right?" demanded Captain Brodst. His heart pounded rapidly in his ears, a lump swelled in his throat. He paced back and forth, and waved a torch haphazardly about in the air, paying little attention to the water and muck that dripped from his uniform. The young Princess Adrina, her face deathlike, was his only concern.

He feared the worst for Adrina as her face grew ashen. He was positive King Andrew would have his head for this. His despair grew, so did his anger and frustration. Again, he yelled at Father Jacob who apparently was not listening to him. "Father, will she be all right?"

Father Jacob had worked frantically ever since Captain Brodst had rescued Adrina from the murky waters of the mire. Although a male, he knew the art of healing well and had attempted to work its miracles on her almost immediately. Yet he was growing annoyed by the captain's repeated inquiries and this distracted him.

"Perhaps, perhaps," he hissed back at the captain, "if you give me some silence!"

Keeper Martin touched a hand to the captain's shoulder and said, "Do not worry so. Father Jacob knows what he is doing. Give him some room and the silence he asks for, then trust in him and Great-Father." Then he returned the captain's cloak and sword belt.

Captain Brodst took the belt and cloak and donned them. He chased off the reassuring hand. He didn't want to be soothed. He wanted Adrina to regain consciousness and to ensure this, he whispered numerous pleas to Great-Father.

There was doubt in Father Jacob's mind as he continued to labor over Adrina, his healing abilities were not as great as those who were of the Mother. Jacob would have offered his soul to have a priestess of the Mother stumble across their path if he hadn't believed that somehow he could save Adrina—after all, she had been in the presage. All he had to do was to overcome his doubt.

Instinctively, Father Jacob had laid Adrina on her side and managed to clear some of the water from her lungs, still she had not regained consciousness, nor did she breathe. Father Jacob could not touch enough of the Mother's will to draw upon her powers to cure. Only after special prayers were sent to Great-Father to give him the extra strength necessary did Jacob begin to chant the incantation—the ancient litany of life and healing. He wouldn't think it odd that fate had brought him to this path until sometime later as he reflected upon this happening.

Erase doubt, he reminded himself, think only of healing and life. He continued the rhythmic chanting.

A noticeable shift swept across Adrina's features, her chest rose once and then fell as her body convulsed. Soon Father Jacob heard the strangled sounds of the girl choking on water still in her lungs. He slapped her back repeatedly and forced her to cough.

Adrina choked on the water she spit up, and gasped frantically for air. She inhaled deeply and rapidly. Violently she vomited the mixture of water and mud she had swallowed—Jacob never broke the rhythmic tone of the litany of life and healing. After a moment, Adrina stopped her convulsing and regained her senses. Tears rolled down her cheeks as she reached up to embrace Father Jacob.

"I'm sorry," she whimpered, "I'm sorry." She closed her eyes briefly against the tears and let the elder hold her.

"Blankets! Get me some blankets, now!" said Father Jacob. He was clearly drained of all his strength. His face was pale and wet with perspiration. He sighed, he had done it, he had succeeded. "We must keep her warm. She will need to get some deep rest soon, and in a warm, comfortable bed."

Silence prevailed for a time afterward as Jacob's words settled on those listening—they must get through this damnable mire and reach the elusive castle somewhere in the distance. Night had settled upon them somewhere during the journey through the mire or perhaps in the frantic moments following Adrina's near fatal accident. Only Father Jacob truly knew how close Adrina had come to death's door, for he was of Great-Father and Great-Father knew all, especially in matters of death.

With unsettling certainty, Father Jacob knew that an unseen evil had been at hand. Great-Father had sensed it and so had he.

Chapter One:
Passage

"We cannot just bed down here surely," came a grumble from a mixture of voices.

Captain Brodst's cold, dark eyes glared back. No further grumblings were made, yet there was truth to be found in those words. All their gear was soaked. Three men had worked furiously for many long minutes to ignite damp kindling and get a small fire started. The meager fire that warmed young Princess Adrina would not last long, and what would they do afterward?

They could not bed down here. The road was narrow and the mire was on both sides of them. Besides, a night in the dampness of the mire and they would *all* catch their death of cold.

Captain Brodst had planned to continue the march for a few hours past sunset and reach Fraddylwicke Castle, but it was already night and the castle was still a half day's march away. Ahead there was a place where hillocks rose out of the mire. Surely there they should have better luck starting a base fire from which they could light the many fires needed for the camp. But that still wouldn't solve their problems, for Captain Brodst knew those shallow hills, there it would be nearly as cold and as damp as if they had bedded down right where they were. No, Adrina needed to sleep in a bed beside a roaring fire, his men needed a place to dry wet clothes and wet gear. Fraddylwicke Castle and its commons was the only place where they'd find both.

Captain Brodst looked to Adrina then turned to one of his sub-commanders.

"Captain Adylton, command of the foot is yours. I want you to keep the men in good spirits and reach the castle as soon as possible. There'll be hot food and fires waiting if I have to rouse every innkeeper's cook within a mile of the castle."

Captain Brodst turned to his second in command. "Captain Trendmore, muster the horse, we ride for Fraddylwicke Castle."

***

The long file was quickly regaining formation. Torches fanned out and faded into the dismal fog. Adrina seemed to be still dazed. She kept repeating, "I'm sorry, I'm sorry," as Captain Brodst picked her up in his arms and carried her to his horse.

A guardsman momentarily held Adrina while the captain mounted, then Captain Brodst took her gently into his arms. While holding reins in one hand, he held her tightly with the opposite arm. Captain Brodst joined the middle of the horse column, Captain Trendmore fell in beside him.

Despite dense fog, Captain Brodst urged the group to maintain a fast pace. They were in a race against time and bone-chilling dampness. The ridesmen feared the captain's wrath, and none offered further complaints. Their thoughts and concerns were also with the young Princess Adrina. She was royalty and thus revered. There were none among the simple men who would not have given his life for hers.

The night air grew steadily colder as the mire seemed to drink in the last remnants of reassuring heat. When mixed with the damp, the chill reached through thick clothing. An uncanny sense of dread hung in the air and Father Jacob wasn't the only one who could feel it now. Soon all longed to reach a place where a hearty fire could be raised and the unchanging darkness of the mire left far behind.

With the changing of temperature toward freezing came a slow, subtle end to the fog. Gradually it faded into small patches of outlying mists and as the night drew on the captain increased the pace accordingly. Oddly, though, a relieved sigh did not pass throughout until much later.

A short distance ahead lurked a series of interconnecting low hills and upon reaching them the captain stopped the group to release the stress from the intense pace. This gave the horses a short break for feed and water, and riders time to stretch sore muscles. Also, Captain Brodst wanted Father Jacob to check Adrina's condition to ensure it had not worsened.

While the good father checked on Adrina, Captain Brodst momentarily stretched tired muscles. He gazed back across the mire they had traversed and into the darkness that surrounded them. He tried to convince himself that Adrina's accident had not changed his plans. His hope was to reach the castle commons in an hour, two at the most. Once inside the castle, Princess Adrina would be safe, and there she would stay. In a few days, when she was well enough to travel, she would continue on to Klaive. He however, could not afford to waste precious days waiting for a recovery only Father Jacob could ensure. Five days, he told himself. Five days to reach Alderan.

Captain Trendmore, who had been checking on the men, returned. "It would seem our plans have changed," he said.

Captain Brodst shook his head, at times it seemed as if Captain Trendmore could read minds. "No, nothing has changed." He wasn't in the mood for a conversation, so he spoke tersely.

"With Princess Adrina in such a state—"

"—You are forgetting one thing, we haven't even reached Fraddylwicke Castle yet. For now, I will change no plans."

"The Prince's party will not leave Quashan' until the Seventhday, that gives us a week to reach our destination. A day's rest will be good for everyone."

"Less than a week. At the rate we are traveling, we are already a day or more behind schedule. We will obtain as many fresh mounts as we can and continue south in the morning as planned, unless I decide otherwise."

"Surely you do not intend to leave the Princess and continue on."

Captain Brodst turned away, ending the conversation.

Father Jacob finished his examination of Adrina. He told Captain Brodst her condition had not worsened. After more blankets were wrapped around her, Captain Brodst gave the order to prepare for movement.

Before Father Jacob went to his mount, he told Captain

Brodst, "Try not to jostle her so. I know you wish to move swiftly, but you must exercise caution. I do not know what bones she may have broken."

"Thank you, Father Jacob, I will try to remember that."

Captain Brodst waited until Jacob was in the saddle then called out, "The princess' condition has not worsened. There is still hope, but we must move swiftly. Pray to Great-Father, all!"

With renewed vigor after the short reprieve and the captain's enthusiastic words, the riders began anew. The ground did not level off immediately after the last of the hills were left behind. Instead it seemed to slope gradually downward, its base enveloped in a bank of swirling mists.

Captain Brodst passed a warning along to the riders at the fore. "Watch the trail before you carefully!"

With great reservation and careful hesitation, they entered the gray veil of dense fog a second time. The captain hoped it would last only until they crossed the shallow point at the bottom of the long downgrade. For an instant he turned his eyes to look down upon Adrina to make sure his heavy woolen cloak was still pulled tightly around her.

"Soon," he said, "soon, we will stop. Rest, princess, rest."

Suddenly the crying whinnies of a frightened mare broke the air followed by the frantic yelling of the lead rider as he jerked harshly on his mount's reins. "Captain Brodst, captain! Quickly!" the rider shouted.

The others behind him came to a similarly abrupt halt. Captain Brodst urged his mount faster and raced to the front of the group. He was amazed at what he saw as he approached the first rider.

Ahead in the distance he could see nothing but water and loose patches of dense fog. The road was gone, apparently washed away. His fears rang true.

A voice reached out into the darkness seeming to stir even the hidden creatures of the mire. "Bring up torches!" Captain Brodst cried out. "Hurry, you louts!"

A large gaggle of men stormed toward the captain. They raised their fiery brands high into the air. The only response to this was a scattered reflection off the water, a dingy yellow mirror of dull orange torch flames.

"It is only an illusion of the fog. The road is washed out at the bottom of the trail nothing more. You there and you, move out!" ordered Captain Brodst.

Those he pointed to shrank back and his scowl deepened.

"Mount and ride out into the water," he ordered again, this time he pointed to two palace guardsmen and made sure he had eye contact with them. "The trail must be there. Find it and be quick about it!"

***

The chosen two entered the dreadful darkness of the lurking waters with reverent care. Movements of their horses were slow and sluggish as the animals fought for every step through the sticky goo of the mire.

They passed through layer upon layer of swirling gray. It seemed dark waters stretched on endlessly before them with no hope of an end. Their mounts began to sink deeper into the muck with each step. Soon the animals, having better sense than the riders, refused to move further without constant coaxing and even then, they became disquieted and whinnied their disapproval.

The chosen two respected the keen sense of their mounts. When the yearning for a retreat out of the gloom became stronger than the urge to continue, they came to a frustrated halt.

They puzzled for a moment over possible solutions, then attempted to maneuver in different directions but to no avail. Their mounts only got more bogged down. Soon they would not be able to escape the mire's yearning grasp. And if strong beasts could not break free neither could simple men. The road simply was not there.

"Cap-tain... Cap-tain Brodst," screamed one of the men. "Sir, there is only water ahead. We are sinking into the mire... We cannot continue."

"You must continue. We must reach the castle... There is a path, find it!"

"But Captain," said the other rider, "we cannot go any farther. We will be lost."

"You must try, there is hope. Do not give up so soon. Push forward!"

The two bravely forced their mounts into movement. With each step the animals sank deeper and deeper into the mud. Soon cold waters lapped at the riders' boots and then there was no retreat backwards or forwards. They were completely stuck.

Kicked, swatted and cursed at, the horses felt the frustration of their riders and it caused them to panic. The scene quickly turned to turmoil, with neither rider retaining a clear mind capable of rational thought. Desperation fed their frenzied movements and their crazed thoughts.

***

Panic-stricken screams reached those waiting behind and created an alarm. No one knew what caused such desperation. Had something as black and as grim as the mire found the unsuspecting two? Was it waiting for them all out there in the swirling gray mists?

Captain Brodst called out, "What has happened? Do you need our assistance?"

He paused for a moment waiting for a response. The shouts continued unabated. He quickly dispatched two additional riders to tread into the murky waters and assist the others. They did as ordered, but with great reservation.

"Try to remain calm," shouted Keeper Martin—he sensed the cause of the panic. "Aid is coming to you."

Captain Brodst nodded in agreement as he also realized what had occurred. He began passing out orders. He told the riders to wait, ordered several squads to come forward and passed the princess into safe hands.

"Ropes," Captain Brodst shouted, "Ropes!"

He untied a rope from around his saddlebag and, after he secured it, threw the coil to the closest rider. "Tie it to your length."

Then he turned to one of his sub-commanders. "Captain Ghenson, throw your rope to the other rider!"

Captain Brodst continued to pass out orders, his mind quick and calculating under pressure.

"I need two more lengths of rope," he said.

Another man handed two ropes to Father Jacob, which he in

turn gave to Captain Ghenson and Captain Brodst to add to their lines for additional distance.

When all was ready, he turned back to the two riders who were awaiting his orders. "Take up the slack, move with caution. When you reach them, toss each a line and tell them to tie it off securely. I pray we can provide them the extra strength necessary to return safely. When you are ready, yell loudly. We will begin to pull on a three count..."

***

One of the trapped guardsmen had lost his torch in the frenzy. The other's had expired and now only darkness remained to add to the worries of their already troubled minds. Slight shifts in the air around them caused their minds to flee in all directions. What could be out there lurking around them unseen and unknown?

Alone and isolated, they searched for any sign or source of light to pierce the blackness. A barely audible splashing, slurping noise crept into range of their listening ears. One of the guards drew his blade and, after a brief moment, the other did the same. In the stillness of their surroundings, the sound seemed to grow in intensity until it became an unnerving clamor.

Two tiny points of light pierced the darkness as a glowing pair of spheres—eyes to the beholders—that grew in intensity with each passing moment. A shrill voice cried out and without heed to the message the trapped two prepared for the end, for they knew it came.

The voice cried out again. "Where are you? Say something, are you there?"

A moment of realization passed between both men. "Over

here, over here! Here we are!" they cried.

The rescuers homed in on the direction of the voices. They saw only darkness and proceeded cautiously. The endless spans of the darkened mire pulled and played upon them, and took them deep into its folds. Soon they too could barely coax their mounts through the muck.

"We cannot reach you!" shouted one of the approaching riders.

His frantic partner screamed, "Where are you? We are sinking!"

Panic spread also to their thoughts. They didn't want to be stuck like the others. They had to escape before the mire swallowed them like it surely would the other two. After they had ensured their own ropes were properly secured they began to shout wildly. Several sharp tugs at the lines caused those waiting to quickly pull them back in.

Not entirely pleased with the performance of the two before him who he now considered cowards, and nearing the end of his patience, Captain Brodst began a thorough chastising. His anger forced him to become irrational. Sword withdrawn, mount turned, eyes glaring, he stared down the first, while he waited for the second to emerge fully from the darkness.

With his free hand, he motioned for them to dismount and step forward. They did so reluctantly.

In a series of lightening swift slashes, Captain Brodst lashed out with his blade, and cropped the lapels from their shoulders. The guardsmen had not flinched at the sight of the captain's blade, yet they had felt its wrath as if it had pierced their hearts.

Pity entered the thoughts of the onlookers, for they all understood the sign and knew it could have just as easily been their own fate. Even Keeper Martin, who was not an initiate, understood the unspoken meaning of the captain's gesture. The two were no longer members of the elite palace guard.

Stripped of the privileges of their rank and all its entitlements, the two nearly wept as they withdrew. Failure was not an easy notion for Captain Brodst to swallow. He sheathed his sword without regrets for his action.

"Give me a torch!" He yelled, his voice boomed. "Tie these ropes off and prepare for my signal... Father Jacob, keep Princess Adrina warm. We are going to get her to the castle if it requires my last breath to do it... Keeper Martin, can I have your long walking stick?"

***

"Hold on, keep talking so I can maintain a bearing on you," Captain Brodst yelled out.

He drove his stallion onward in the direction of the screaming voices.

"Where are your torches?"

"One is lost and the other is burnt out."

"If you have some flint lay a spark to it. It may yet burn."

Even in the fog, Captain Brodst saw the light the tiny sparks afforded as they were struck and knew he was close. Progress was becoming arduous now and he had a difficult time persuading his mount to move ahead, but he did not retreat like the others. Inch by inch, his mount crept closer to the trapped riders.

"Find a dried cloth in your bags. Anything dry. Tie it to the top of the torch. Then lay a spark to it!"

Captain Brodst waited for a response. A shout of hooray

erupted from the two as they managed to light the torch at long last and confidence began to replace their unease.

Captain Brodst now had a beacon to follow toward the two. He changed his harshness to gentleness, and soothed his horse while he urged it to trudge through murky waters. The stallion, responding to his master's faith, pushed onward using its powerful legs to advance slowly and methodically.

Captain Brodst readied the rope as he approached. An ecstatic cheer erupted from the hapless two as the first line was caught in yearning hands.

Captain Brodst untied the rope from his saddle horn and tugged the line sharply three times to signal those waiting to start pulling. The slack was quickly taken up as the rope went taunt, the initial strain audible in the air as a loud twang that continued as a stretching noise caused from the heavy tension in the line.

Horse and rider strained as one, yearning to be free from the unwanted grasp. Instinctively, the horse fought to be free as much as the rider wanted to be free, its heavy breathing and the painstaking plodding of each step it took clearly audible.

Sufficiently free, the first man untied the line and pulled it in several yards to throw it back to Captain Brodst who was now fixed approximately midway between the two. It took several attempts before the rope reached the captain and when it finally did, he relayed it to the second man.

Knowingly, Captain Brodst kept his mount moving so that it would not sink too far into the muck of the mire. Once the second rider was at a safe point, Captain Brodst instructed him to make a loop and throw the line back. He secured it tightly to his saddle horn and then to the astonishment of the receding two who were moving back to the safety of firm ground, Captain Brodst turned and plunged deeper into the quagmire.

Defeat was another word he frowned upon.

His scowl was now plastered to his face in thick folds. "Think lightly," he whispered to his mount, "we will find a way."

Initially, he tried to circle around the area where the others had been stuck. Unfortunately, he was caught up in the same sinkhole they had been stuck in. He probed with the keeper's long stick. The search for a spot that was not excessively soft told him he had to retreat in the direction he had come from.

Undaunted by the small setback, he made the detour and then pushed on. He attempted to go around in the opposite direction, and moved outward laterally to the right until he found a spot where he could press forward.

Much to his relief he came upon a tiny spot of land, an island in the middle of the muck, a minute area a mere five feet across and three feet wide, but it was a hard surface from which he could maneuver. Hiding his elation as reservation returned, he stifled a shout for joy. His exhausted steed was rewarded with generous strokes and a brief reprieve.

One last time, he plunged into the muck of the mire, and after only a short struggle again to the right across a small patch of dank swamp, he found the road. In a soft, steady voice he whispered, "Hold on young princess. I promise you'll soon rest in a warm, warm bed."

The captain started to call out to those behind. "A warm bed awaits!" he intended to say, but a faint sloshing, slurping noise caught his trained ear, and no words escaped his lips.

He turned in time to see a dim figure emerge from the gray of the fog. Instinctively he dropped the walking stick, his hand going to the hilt of his long sword, and his heart skipping a beat before he recognized the once grim shadow. He raised a hand in confused salutation.

"Captain, why did you leave ranks?" he asked.

Chapter Two:
Past Thoughts

Hot, it's so hot...

Endless waiting played heavily on Seth's faith. Yet he knew it was faith that he must maintain, for there was nothing else. Only Mother-Earth would carry them to safety or deliver them from life.

Ah, please... please... make the sun go away... make it end...

A full day sun blossomed overhead. The struggle to keep squinted eyes open was borne. Once closed under the beating sun, blisters would return and with them infection, and then eyes might open no more. The ruinous combination of sun and salt water had already desiccated and blistered his body, yet it was his eyes that seemed his most sacred pride.

Seth struggled to his knees. He tested the strength of the pieces of ropes and tattered clothing that held the raft together. Salt water despoiled them. Still, they held well. *Thank you...*

A sudden tremor in his mind sent Seth's thoughts careening outward. *Bryan!* Seth called out.

He perceived no return response, though he could feel the

other's anguish.

Oh please… please, hold on…

Seth carefully removed the cap from the last water bag they possessed and put a single droplet to his own parched lips.

Give me strength… He wanted more, he wanted every drop the bottle contained. *Give me strength…*

The water's caress as it moistened his lips caused a shiver throughout his body. The yearning for more increased, yet he could not, *would not*, allow himself to partake of it.

His hands were shaking. *Give me strength…* He implored.

Seth lowered the water bag. He reached over to where Bryan lay, and cradled his companion's head upward. Slowly and painstakingly, he dropped the precious liquid to Bryan's lips, and savored every drop as if it touched his own lips. He continued to drop the water to Bryan's lips, drop by precious drop, until the brother could swallow. Afterward, he did the same for Galan.

Bryan's and Galan's faces were covered with sun blisters, as was his own, but his thoughts were only for his fellows. *Two must survive no matter the cost,* he whispered to himself, *two must survive—* Queen Mother's last words of warning to him. Delirium enveloped his thoughts and the words echoed through his mind. Somehow he must shield them, somehow they must all survive…

***

More long hours under the burning sun did little for Seth's clarity of mind. He was nearing total delirium. The only thought that kept him near sanity was the one single thought that had kept him through the last three hours. *Two must survive, two must survive no matter the cost,* went the echo in his mind. Surely some time ago he had ceased thinking it, yet the echo still clung to his mind.

With great persistence, Seth moved from a sitting position to a kneeling position—waves shifting the raft and his fatigue made the small accomplishment a difficult chore. He held there motionless for a moment and tried to recall why he had risen to his knees. Then, after a lengthy pause, he sank back down to his haunches. There must have been something he had wanted to do, but what, he couldn't recall.

Two must survive, he whispered.

Weary, Seth slumped down onto his side. He closed and shielded tired eyes, using the tattered shards of a once magnificent cloak to mask his face. For what seemed hours, the ceaseless up and down swaying of the raft lulled him. By luck or fate, or perhaps a little help from Great-Father, Seth managed to focus his will, though only for an instant. He reached outward with his mind trying desperately to reach a knowing consciousness. He found none.

Yet, the momentary clarity of mind also allowed him to concentrate. Surely there was an answer to their dilemma. He pondered this. Something had gone wrong from the start, but *what* had it been. Had there been a traitor among them? Was there a traitor among them now? Was it Bryan or Galan?

No, paranoia. Seth dismissed the idea of a traitor. No one of the Brotherhood would ever betray Queen Mother—*Sathar,* whispered his conscience. *No, Sathar betrayed all. Survival is keyed to the past, the answer is there, if only I can find it.*

Exhausted, Seth started to drift off to sleep and was quickly lost to his dreams. Dreams in which he could replay events that had unfolded against them.

No longer was he in his beloved homeland, surrounded by the peace and serenity of Queen Mother. Now he was thrust out into the strange and cruel world, *into an unknown fate.* Only Great-Father knew how the long struggle would end.

His mind wandered further, and floated through delirium to mixed conscious thought. He began to think back, *back to the time before they had left their homeland.* At first, in this mixed-up delusion that to him seemed real, Seth heard only the voices, his and hers. Yet, as his thoughts cleared and he entered a deeper dream-state, he pieced together disconnected thought without much detail.

It was to this at first colorless world of dream, with only the voices, that he fled.

***

Quickly, Brother Seth. You must wake now or it will be too late! said a voice entering Seth's dream.

All thoughts of sleep were instantly gone. The voice sent a shiver careening down Seth's spine.

Quickly, quickly now, the voice hastened.

Suddenly he was unsure whether the voice was within or without. Was it his own mind that called out the warning, or another?

A shifting of the raft caused Seth to open his eyes. *Was the voice of alarm within or without?*

Seth stepped back into the dream-thought, which was difficult but successfully managed. He ran from his room, down of series of twisting halls and into the great monolithic entry hall. He slowed his pace here to a stately walk. After he had crossed the hall, he descended wide translucent steps of alabaster into the great open courtyard that spread out in gothic proportions in front of him.

This is why I have chosen you, Brothers of the Red, he called out, greeting those already assembled. He spoke powerfully now into the minds of the chosen few. *You were each hand-picked for the task that lies ahead. Queen Mother has spoken and her protectors have listened. Go now to the harbor, Sailmaster Cagan awaits you.*

Seth inspected each as they departed the courtyard. He stopped the last brother, and chased a whisper of thought after her. *Brother Galan, I had wished you to remain here leading the Red in my stead but it could not be so.*

Galan turned and the two locked eyes in a deep drinking gaze that spoke volumes. Her open thoughts streamed to his mind. She was remembering the kiss of many days ago. The meaning of it still confused her.

Shifting on one of his heels, Seth turned about and marched back up the long alabaster stair into the monolithic entry hall and swiftly along it. Queen Mother had retired to a meditation room and to this is where Seth hastened. But Seth did not find Queen Mother there, and it wasn't until many precious minutes later that he considered checking High Hall.

Queen Mother was seated at her place in the middle of the hall, eyes directed straight at him. Seth said, *We leave now, Queen Mother.*

Yes, I know, she imparted softly, yet forcefully. *May Mother-Earth protect all her children who must now leave their home to journey to the world of Man. May the Father guide you on your journey to safety.*

Beckoned by feelings mixed in with the words, Seth looked into Queen Mother's eyes. He had been trembling though he hadn't known it until her soft eyes forced calm into him. *Good-bye, my Queen. We will succeed in this endeavor. We will bring word to the Alder King and persuade him to join our cause. As I have sworn my duty, nothing shall stop me from completing this.*

It was difficult to stare into eyes with such emotion for any length of time, yet when Seth attempted to look away, he was drawn back again by her words and her thoughts. *I have great faith in you, Brother Seth, though I regret your having to make this journey. Alas, all is set in motion. There can be no turning back now. It is up to fate and faith to bring you back safely to our shores.*

I have no regrets, Queen Mother. We will succeed.

Then by my leave, go swiftly, said the Queen as she touched her hand to Seth's brow. She left her index finger lighted there while she said these words, *and this, I whisper only to your mind my son. I as Queen Mother can see shadings of what is yet to come. While I am powerless to stop what has been set in motion, I can say this. You must always be prepared for the unexpected. Never let down your guard. You must accept what you alone are fated to do. Always retain your faith, never let it dwindle...*

Never let it dwindle, repeated Seth.

...Always make it burn brightly as a red-hot ember of your being. Your faith will shelter you. Fare-thee-well my son, and remember that above all else, two must survive the journey, for only one will be able to return to our shores...

Never let it dwindle, repeated Seth as he turned away.

***

Waves beneath the raft shifted and just as his thoughts were coming to a clear, full focus, Seth was jolted from his slumber. He opened bleary eyes to a night sky. He did not marvel at the arrival of darkness. The night sky only meant cruel heat was gone and bitter cold had replaced it.

He was thankful that Bryan and Galan were soundly sleeping. They had survived yet another day beneath the untiring fury of the day sky.

He opened the water skin and put several droplets to his lips. He could have easily finished that last bit of water in the container. It would have only taken a second more. Momentarily, he reveled in the fantasy of it slipping coolly down his throat. The fact that his throat was swollen and every such swallow would have brought sure pain did not taint the longing.

Give me strength, he implored.

Only as he raised the container back to his lips did he find restraint. *Thank you...*

Two must survive, went the ceaseless echo in his mind. He turned his eyes back to the dark waters and a thought from the dream found him. *The mind shield.* The mind shield could resist his probing thoughts. Anyone could be lurking out there in the darkness, waiting just beyond the next crest or trough.

High Hall, why High Hall? Seth thought suddenly, though he didn't dwell on this long. He was elated. Keys beyond the confusion in his mind could be found. *Bryan, Galan!*

He had considered the others a moment ago, though the thought had slipped away before he had a chance to focus on it. *Galan, Bryan?* he called out again.

Neither stirred.

A panicked probing assured him they were alive, although he didn't like the weakness that had come from Bryan and it worried him. Convinced that in order to survive the journey he must lose no more of his companions, Seth was prepared to go to any length to ensure their survival. He would have slashed his own wrists and fed them from the blood that oozed from the open gash if he could have. In the *very* real delirium of his mind, this notion was suddenly appealing, until he realized it would quicken his own passage from life. And life, especially one's own, was sacred.

Suddenly he wished he had learned more about the sea. He knew little of the creatures that lurked beneath the dark waters, only that at night he saw them, the ones called krens with the high dorsal fins, circling round and round their tiny raft. When he had been stronger he had chased them away by sending harsh emotions into their underdeveloped brains. Now he was too weak to attempt this—and nearly too weak to care at all.

Somewhere in the convoluted corners of his mind, he made a connection between the circling predator and Bryan. Suddenly he remembered the water bag still clutched in his upturned hand. He awoke Bryan and forced the brother to drink a few precious drops, but no more.

Do not waste brother, you need this more than I. You must live… came the shallow whisper into his mind, the voice was Bryan's.

Drink, I will not tolerate nonsense.

Afterward Seth gave Galan an equal portion of the water. *Drink, drink,* he said to Galan. *The supply of water is almost spent, soon we will all be without its life giving essence…*

Although his teachings and his faith told him otherwise, he felt completely responsible for the fate of his two companions. If he had but one wish, he would do something, anything that would ease their suffering.

It is time you saved your strength, imparted Galan.

Surprised by the voice, for he had been sure his thoughts were sealed, Seth apologized. *I am sorry Brother Galan. I did not mean to trouble you with open thought.*

Seth, you know better than that. Our fate is predestined, you cannot alter it. You cannot stop the inevitable, you cannot hold back the winds, or the looming hands of fate...

Seth listened to her words yet he did not accept them. The weight of guilt had already scarred him.

Sleep well my Galan, he said, although he doubted Galan had heard him for she was already gathered in a heavy sleep. The presence of the Father faintly came to Seth, as he, too, slipped quickly back to sleep and delirium. His dreams of remembrance grew surprisingly richer.

Two must survive, echoed once more in his thoughts, just before the dreams gathered full force.

***

The first shafts of light from an early morning sun shot over the horizon in the East. The light touched the haze of Seth's mind and caused him to rub his burning eyes. A dry yawn issued from his mouth, and then with one partially unclenched eye, he squinted toward the brightness.

It will be a clear day.

Seth both welcomed the sun's warmth to end the night's cold and feared its erosion of their bodies. For Seth, the days were longer than the nights and, upon reflection, he did indeed prefer the night despite the often bitter cold.

Time passed. The sun seemed to wither and weaken Seth even

more this day. The dryness and excruciating pain of his throat aroused him to its swelling—it was nearly swollen shut. He attempted to squeeze down a lump of dry, pasty spittle, and cried out in a muffled whimper as he did this.

So much water around me and none to drink.

Their small supply of fresh water was nearly exhausted and this was now the only concern in his frazzled mind. *Seawater.* It was all around him and he could drink none of it.

Why can it not rain Father?

Still unconcerned for himself, Seth first touched a few precious drops of moisture to Galan's lips then covered her face and arms again with the tatters of his robe. He drank then, a little more than he should have, barely getting the drops to slide down his aching throat. Then Seth gave Bryan the last few drops the water bag contained.

Is it all for nothing Father?

The day turned to night and back again to day. Seth felt the vitality within him ebb. His consciousness fell to total decay. He could no longer focus his will to maintain him which frustrated him utterly. The forces of nature were all around him, yet he, Seth, First of the Red, could not touch them. He was losing himself and his center. Soon he would slip away to a peaceful bliss that he would have welcomed only a few short days ago. But now he had struggled too long to give in, fought too hard to give up.

Great-Father, is that you? Have you come to gather me home? What did I do wrong?... I do not wish to go... I could not have stopped the ambush... I... I... did not know. No... I cannot fail. I... I must think. I must focus...

ഇറ The Kingdoms & The Elves ഇറ

***

The sun was mid way in the sky before Seth finally came back from the endless world of gray delirium and dream. Visions of ships sinking into the dark, waiting waters that surrounded him even now, slowly fell from his eyes—*so much needless loss.*

A light breeze played soothingly across Seth's tormented skin. Hidden behind a murky cloudbank, a pale sun looked so distant and harmless, yet its ill effects had whittled away his body and his strength slowly and effectively.

Rain may come, Seth mused. If rain came, it may just save them. Then again, the storm unleashed with the rains could drown them just as easily.

Hours diminished to the pace of agonizing seconds and heartbeats. Ignoring the hunger pains in his clenched and swollen stomach, the brittle dryness of his lips and the tremendous aching of his brutalized body, Seth attempted to center his thoughts.

He knew somewhere in his teachings there must be an answer to their dilemma. He searched the indexes of his mind. A wish sprang to mind, a wish that he had learned more about seamanship from Cagan, the crafty sea captain who he had known since childhood and who, since his childhood, had commanded the Queen's own fleet. Such learning would have proven a worthwhile investment, yet then he had not had time for such foolish endeavors.

Seth felt a faint prick of pain in his mind. He strained to focus his thoughts. As he did this, sadness swept over him and in an unexplainable way Seth knew something was wrong. *Is someone in my thoughts?*

A gentle whisper entered Seth's mind.

Yes? he answered.

If I told you I was afraid, what would you say? asked Galan.

Seth reached out for Galan's hand and took it in his. *We all have our fears, Brother Galan. It is not wrong to fear what we do not know.*

I fear death, said Galan sending feelings of hopelessness along with the words. *I fear in death I will find only longing and emptiness.*

Great-Father will not forsake— Seth felt another prick of pain in his mind. *—Is that you, Brother Galan?*

You are wrong. For those who have failed, there can be no joy in the next life. The voice nearly inaudible in their minds and edged with bitterness was Bryan's.

Seth disagreed. *While blood courses through your veins it tells you that you live.*

I died long ago, said Bryan.

Bryan's sadness flowed strongly to Seth. It encompassed him and the whole of their bantam raft. Then Seth felt pain again. *What are you doing in my thoughts?*

I'm dying Seth.

Dying? Seth wheeled about the raft wildly. Frantically he searched for the precious water bag. His aim was to pour its every drop down Bryan's throat in the desperate hope that it alone would keep him. It was then Seth remembered they had no more water. He had used the last of it.

No Brother, said Seth. *It is not time, it is not your time! You must hold strong, you cannot desert us. We need you, I need you. There is so much, so very much...*

Bryan didn't or couldn't answer.

Bryan, please answer me... There is a way, there must be a way... The dream, the dream, the answers are there, please hold on. I will find them... I will.

Seth's eyes flashed to his wrists. The blood coursing through his veins gave him life, it would give Bryan life.

Go ahead Seth, whispered the voice, Bryan's voice in his mind. *Two must live.*

No Seth, it is already too late for him. It is not yet our time. Mother-Earth still has plans for us.

Galan cried out in sudden pain.

Go ahead Seth, it is your fault I die. You owe me your life. You bring shame and dishonor to our kind.

Paralyzing anguish shot through Seth's mind. *No, Seth, it is his time. Our time is yet to be destined.*

Again, Galan cried out in pain. Hands suddenly gripped Seth's throat.

Bryan, what are you doing? Remember, you pulled me from the water, you saved my life—Ga-lan, he's choking... me—Bryan are you mad?

You still don't understand, do you Seth? Bryan squeezed harder.

The hands still at his throat, Seth struggled wildly to his knees. Galan made her move and hit Bryan from the side.

Seth found Bryan unexpectedly strong and only with Galan's help was he able to break the hands from his throat. Together, wobbly and barely able to keep their feet, Seth and Galan fended off Bryan's blows. Seth ducked to dodge a blow. Galan lunged at Bryan, and knocked him off his feet. Together they fell into the sea.

Seth let out a high-pitched cry of anguish. He scrambled to the edge of the raft.

Galan and Bryan broke the surface. They were still struggling. On his belly now, Seth reached out to Galan. He felt the tip of her fingers touch his. Then Bryan pulled Galan under with him for what seemed the final time.

Seth lay still. He stared into the dark waters through red and burning eyes. Despair ravaged his heart.

Chapter Three:
Awakening

"Isador?... Isador, I saw him. I saw him!" screamed Adrina, as she roused from a feverish state. "He is hurting. He needs our help!".

"Princess, it was only a dream," said an alarmed Father Jacob. The sound of Adrina's voice had startled him. He took the moist towel from her brow, dipped it into the cold water of the basin beside him, then reapplied it to her forehead. The fever must have finally broken, he thought.

"We must hurry," continued Adrina heatedly.

"It was only a dream," repeated Father Jacob. He patiently dabbed the girl's forehead with the cold towel.

"His eyes were the bluest blue. He spoke to me in the dream." Adrina lurched up in bed, then after putting feet to floor, she stood. She looked around the unfamiliar room and stopped. A puzzled frown crossed her face. "Fa-ther Ja-cob?... Where am I and how did I get here?"

The room started to swirl around her, twisting and turning

round and round. Adrina began to lose her balance. She fought to steady herself. Father Jacob caught her and ferried her back into bed. She looked up at him, her eyes wide and imploring, and said, "We must leave now. I know where he is. Just as the lady said, the ship did not reach Alderan."

Father Jacob was sure Adrina was talking gibberish again. She had said many things in her fevered state. "Child you must rest. Tomorrow will bring a new day. The others will return soon enough."

"No, you don't understand. Get Keeper Martin. He understands, he will listen to me."

"I am afraid they have already departed. You have been asleep for quite some time. Now please get some rest, my child," said Jacob. He pulled heavy blankets up around Adrina to keep the girl warm.

Adrina wanted to say something else but Jacob silenced her and again bade her to sleep. As Jacob turned away, Adrina grabbed his arm and squeezed as hard as she could to gain his attention. She didn't want to sleep—at least, not yet. Once she had his attention, she stared straight into his eyes and stated in a calm, portentous manner, "When did they leave?... We must go now before it is *too* late."

Father Jacob was taken aback by her words, something told him to listen to her. "Slow down, Adrina. I am afraid I don't understand. Tell me of the dream?"

After a brief moment of silence, Adrina said, "It was in my dreams, father. I saw Prince William and he spoke to me. I know where he is and he urgently needs our help... There is something wrong."

"You are full of fever. Prince William is in Alderan. No harm could have befallen him there."

Adrina closed her eyes for a moment though she did not let go of Jacob's arm. "No, the ship from Wellison did not complete the journey. The voices, the message, Father Jacob, it was all *real*... You must believe me. If only Keeper Martin were here. *He* would understand."

"I believe you young princess," said Father Jacob, "but you are in no condition to travel."

Adrina regarded Father Jacob with serious eyes. "Are you patronizing me?"

"You close your eyes and rest now. I'll see if I can arrange travel accommodations." Jacob nodded his head wearily. He wasn't convinced it was a good idea to leave Fraddylwicke Castle. He departed Adrina's chamber with troubled thoughts filling his mind. His hope was that the girl would be fast asleep when he returned.

***

Adrina gathered her strength and sat up. She stretched her arms and her sore back with a hefty, stretching-yawn. A few minutes passed without movement as she attempted to shake dizziness away. Eventually the room did stop moving. She slipped over to the side of the bed and placed her feet on the floor.

Carefully she reached out, grasped her boots, then slipped her feet into them. A bit wobbly, she stood up and looked about the chamber. Bright daylight pouring in through a terraced doorway instantly caught her attention. She walked out onto the balcony and squinted at the bright orange of the sun, which to her astonishment was midway in the sky.

She rushed back into the chamber, which seemed suddenly dark. She stumbled. She had moved too fast. She pressed up against the frame of the door and held herself there for several long breaths while her eyes slowly readjusted to the dimness of the interior.

After a quick scan for belongings in the unfamiliar room, she prepared to leave. Instinctively she checked her hair in the large mirror that stood beside the door on her way out. Her hair was a mess. She ran her fingers through it to straighten it. Abruptly she stopped what she was doing and stared at her reflection. Something wasn't right. It took her a moment to realize she was wearing a nightgown. To have put her boots on while she still wore bed clothes. Whatever was she thinking?

She wasn't thinking.

Her head ached on one side—a dull throbbing that numbed her awareness—as if she had been kicked, and a large swollen area on the right side of her skull attested to this fact. She touched it gingerly and winced.

Think clearly, think clearly. She tensed up and took a couple of deep breaths, trying to concentrate. All right, now what was I doing?

It took her a moment to remember and only after staring into the mirror again did she finally realize what she needed to do next.

"Riding clothes, riding clothes," she muttered to herself.

At the opposite end of the large chamber was a partial wall-divider, which she finally realized was where the dressing area must be. I knew that. Where was my brain?

Adrina touched the lump on the side of her head. She screamed out, "Ouch!" Her brain was there—in pain.

It was a slow methodical shuffle to the divider and even slower changing into her riding clothes that were clean and thankfully dry—she recalled now that they had been wet, that she had been wet.

A dull thump sounded at the door as she was dressing and Adrina shouted, "Just a moment—"

"Oo, ouch!" she moaned. Her head throbbed with pain. No more shouting.

It took a few more careful minutes before Adrina finished dressing and walked over to open the door. She opened it to find Father Jacob standing solemnly, a deep-set frown on his face.

"I was hoping you would be fast asleep when I returned," he said, as he stepped into the chamber.

"No such luck," said Adrina with heedful volume so as not to cause her head to pound any more than it already did.

"You are still flushed with fever. A day's delay will cause little harm. I am concerned about your health, child, more than anything else. That was a nasty fall. You need to rest."

"There will be plenty of time to rest later, Father Jacob."

Father Jacob started to reply. Adrina reached out and took his hand in hers. "I must do this, Father Jacob." She spoke with sincerity.

Adrina started to lead Jacob into the hall and as he stepped back into the corridor, he stopped. "Wait a minute, am I crazy? I didn't want to do this, but if I have to… Get back into that bed this instant, you will sleep!"

Adrina stepped deftly passed Father Jacob. "This will not wait, father. He is dying, I know it. Did you know—" Hesitant, Adrina stopped herself from saying anything more.

Jacob took a step toward her. "Go on," he said.

"It was only the voice at first, calling out, but then I started to see things. It was as if I were traveling a great distance. There was so much I know I saw that I cannot recollect, so much, Father Jacob... The vision first led me out to sea, then to the southern coast—"

"Did you?" asked Jacob, "No, of course you didn't, did you?"

"Did I what, Father Jacob?"

"At any rate, we cannot leave until Captain Brodst recovers. I would not hear the last of it if I left him in Fraddylwicke Castle with the Baron and Baroness."

Adrina nearly fell as the words hit her. Father Jacob fought to ferry her back to bed but she wouldn't let him. "Who leads the column to Alderan?"

"The second in command *was* Captain Trendmore. He assumed command after Captain Brodst's unfortunate accident. He waited until late this morning, but couldn't wait any longer. With Prince Valam's arrival in Alderan in three days, he had to leave. It will take a miracle—" Jacob glanced heavenward. "—for them to make that march in three days. I am sure Captain Brodst said it would take at least five."

Adrina's face turned deathly pale. Now she understood why the detachment had turned south for Quashan'. Now she understood why so much was at stake in Alderan. "Prince Valam is to meet the ship from Wellison, the ship carrying Prince William?"

〄 The Kingdoms & The Elves 〄

The lady's words flooded into Adrina's mind and piece by piece she started to put the puzzle together. *The ship from Wellison has a most precious cargo, the heir to the throne of Sever. At this very moment King Charles lies dying in his bed… King Jarom sees himself seated in the throne room of Imtal Palace. He means to plunge the kingdoms into war. To be sure, he will use the death of Charles and the fears of the heir to his own ends…*

Adrina decided right then to confide in Father Jacob. She recounted the meetings with the strange lady. She told him of the first meeting in the palace tower at Imtal and the second meeting in the forest on the night of the heavy rains.

As Adrina watched, it was clear a flood of awareness swept over Father Jacob. He was silent for a time then he mumbled words Adrina barely understood. "This is the very message Great-Father sent—the message I have puzzled over these long past days."

"Father Jacob, are you all right? Is there something I can do for you?"

"Just let me stand here a moment, child." Father Jacob paused, took a deep breath then added, "On second thought, let's sit. Perhaps over on the bed…"

Father Jacob regarded Adrina with marvel. "I told no one about the voices and the portentous messages that brought me to Imtal Palace on a dark night, what seemed so long ago. I did not even tell the cunning Keeper Martin… Great-Father does sometimes work in mysterious ways. Messages in dreams are not uncommon and the Lore Keepers often use them for long communication."

Father Jacob again became quiet and the wrinkles around his

eyes grew thick. "You are right, child," said Father Jacob at long last, "we cannot wait. May Great-Father speed us on to Alderan..."

***

Adrina approached the low portcullis that separated thick walls midway along the castle's southerly bastion. She continued past it to the stables where a stately wagon was being prepared. The Lord and Lady Fraddylwicke had chased after her every step of the way from the inner courtyard to the wall, but neither the baroness' "Your Highness, please, the tea is ready," or the baron's "The wagon would have been ready in another hour," would slow her down.

Yesterday it had been the baron who had convinced Father Jacob that they should not leave the castle until this morning. It was true that by the time preparations had been made and they were ready to leave it was late afternoon, but there still had been a few hours of daylight left. What harm would a night in the swamp have brought? This morning, the baroness was dead set on having tea after breakfast. Who drinks tea at daybreak?

Adrina cast a glum stare behind her. Father Jacob hurried along beside the baron, and Adrina heard him again speaking an apology. "It seems we must leave at once on an urgent matter," he was saying. "Please give the message I left for Captain Brodst to him as soon as he wakes. You have been most gracious hosts. His Majesty will surely hear of this."

"Raise the portcullis," Adrina screamed to the guards inside the gatehouse.

"The wagon is most splendid," Jacob said, seemingly to drown out Adrina's words.

No doubt, Lord Fraddylwicke had chosen the stately wagon with its four-horse team with clear purpose. Adrina knew this was meant as a symbol both of his wealth and of his generosity, which he hoped would be relayed to King Andrew. She didn't find it odd that she could so intensely dislike a man who she had only met yesterday evening.

Behind her, Adrina heard men shouting, she looked back to the outer courtyard to see a small contingent of foot soldiers mustering. Adrina stopped and whirled about to face the baron. "A gaggle of foot soldiers will only slow us down. We need the wagon and the provisions you promised, nothing more. Tell them to return to their duties."

"Your Highness, I must object," Baron Fraddylwicke said. "I must see to your protection. The swamp is no place for a lady such as yourself to be alone."

Adrina started respond, but Father Jacob spoke first. "He is right, Princess Adrina. It would be best to have an escort."

"Fine, if they are to come along, have them mount up. They can ride, yes?"

"I am afraid—" Adrina held her breath. The baron was fond of those three words. "—that the scant few animals that remain are ill-fit for riding. Your Captain Trendmore took every horse in Fraddylwicke. Strangest thing, I told him I needed mounts for the King's messengers—you see, usually we trade out on a one-for-one basis—but he said he wanted them all and would keep his. Even sent men about the countryside. He left nary one behind. It is only by the grace of Great-Father that my personal team remains."

Adrina started to say, "Great-Father had nothing to do with it," but then realized that it was fortunate the baron had hidden the animals away. Her irritation with the pompous baron decreased. She bit her cheek and smiled.

"That was a wise decision," she said, "my father, the King, will surely hear how you have helped me, for I will tell him personally. The foot soldiers stay here, however."

Baron Fraddylwicke's face suddenly seemed to glow and the baroness touched her kerchief to her eye. "As you wish," the baron said.

Father Jacob nodded approval and helped Adrina climb into the wagon.

***

The four-horse team eagerly responded to Jacob's guiding hands. At first the gentle countryside that encompassed Fraddylwicke Castle greeted them, but this was a short-enjoyed oasis in the midst of surrounding mires, and after only an hour of riding the roads began to slope gradually downward to be reclaimed by the wetlands.

Instantly Adrina and Jacob felt moisture in the air and smelled pungent odors of stagnant waters. Fortunately, the roads leading away from the castle in this section of the lowlands were well reinforced. The main road was built up a full three feet above the waiting waters. Adrina marveled at the feat of ingenuity and determination it had taken to build such an access way.

A dreary haze hung over the mire, giving it unparalleled uncanniness. This, when added to the sense of foreboding Adrina felt, put her at considerable unease. She puzzled over a great many things, especially how Prince Valam fit into all this. To be sure, they must reach Alderan before her brother's arrival. They also needed to catch up to the column and warn them, but what would they tell them to watch out for? And what of Prince William? If his ship had not arrived in Alderan, why had no messages been sent? Why in the dream was he in such pain? And why had he stared at her so?

As she tried to think about all this, Adrina's head began to throb, the pain becoming so intense that all her thoughts eventually fell away. Ahead in the distance lay disparate crossroads that led to tiny villages whose buildings dotted the landscape. Mounted on top of tiny cross-sections of land that were barely habitable, the villages seemed much like the swamp's scattered weeping willow trees, waiting to be reclaimed someday by the dank surrounding waters.

Hoping to rid herself of throbbing headache and troubled thoughts, Adrina turned to Father Jacob. And though he seemed deep in his own concerns, she endeavored to spark a conversation with him.

"It all looks so lonely, does it not, Father Jacob?" said Adrina, her voice mixing in with the thump-roll, thump-roll of the wagon's wheels. "I'm curious about Lord Fraddylwicke, such a grand castle in the middle of all this waste. Everything so well maintained, these roads as well. The villages we pass are impoverished. With tithing to the temples there can be little wealth left to tax. Does the Baron tax in blood?"

Jacob was slow to reply, but it seemed clear as he began that he grasped Adrina's intent, which was to rid their minds of troubled thoughts for a time. "I find these lands curious as well. Only the southern portion of the mire remains populated, you know. During the Great Wars, the castle was a major strategic point for King Jarom the First, but now it serves no useful purpose. There are other safeguarded passages to the southlands.

"The wars lasted generations and it does seem odd that anyone would chose to stay in so desolate a place afterward. Perhaps they stay simply because it is their ancestral home."

"Perhaps," said Adrina.

"In a way I pity them, and not only because the desolation and isolation they endure seem overbearing. Also because generations of war and life in such a place left behind a bitter and superstitious people. Their ancestors are King Jarom's Blood Soldiers. Too brutal and uncivilized for the civilized world that emerged after the Great Wars and too many to exterminate, they are all but forgotten about by both the kingdom that gave them birth and the kingdom that conquered them."

"Blood Soldiers, why have I never heard about them?"

"You won't find anything I've just told you in any book in Imtal, this I assure, though Keeper Martin would verify the history. Yet, it is perhaps best they remain forgotten."

Father Jacob whipped the reins held tightly in his hands. Adrina took this as a sign to change the topic of their conversation. "Father Jacob, how long will it take to reach the coast?"

Jacob thought about it for a short time and then responded, "Great-Father willing and if we pray very hard and drive the horses as much as we dare, we might be able to reach it by midmorning tomorrow."

"And Alderan?"

"Early the day after, if we pray."

"Then we will pray," said Adrina matter-of-factly.

Weariness swept over Adrina like a storm. Her face turned pale and though she fought to stay awake, sleep came.

The wagon continued to speed along the trail . Jacob's thoughts were on the wagon and the trail ahead. It took great care to hold the trail steadily at the increased speed. He was so engrossed in his concentration that he did not notice Adrina's state. He only heard the horses' hooves thundering along the trail.

The sky above grew overcast, the winds began to pick up, and an ill feeling intensified in Father Jacob's gut. His intuition told him a heavy storm was approaching. He cast silent prayers to Great-Father to protect them from the rains and to allow them to complete their journey unscathed.

But it was a losing affray that was being conducted against the squall in the good priest's mind. The clouds overhead turned dark and callous quickly. Jacob felt their presence as an evil spirit invading his privacy.

The air turned cold. The first droplets of rain fell. Jacob beat at the reins with increasing ferocity matched by the increasing fury of the wind. Sprinkles of rain thrashed against them, then the downpour began.

Jacob secured the top button of his cloak and turned up the high collar. "There are extra blankets in the rear—" Jacob stopped cold, the words frozen on his lips. Suddenly he saw Adrina, her face colorless, deathly pale, and fear entered his thoughts and took control. He commanded the horses to halt.

With trembling hands, he reached out and touched Adrina's face. It was cold, sticky wet with perspiration and rain. He removed the extra blankets from the rear of the wagon and bundled Adrina in them. Then he drove the horses onward, faster and faster. Somewhere ahead he hoped to find a crossroads that would lead to a village.

Anxiety swept over him as they sped along the road. He chastised himself repeatedly in his mind. Rain began to fall in mighty torrents as the storm engulfed them. Wind, rain and diminished visibility made the road treacherous but Jacob did not slow the horses. He continued to push the wagon to its limits.

Lost to the frenzy of the moment, his mind stressed and incapable of clear thought, Jacob panicked. Frantically he scanned ahead, his thoughts running in a hundred different directions and many times he glanced worriedly at Adrina.

Jacob drove the team on, urging the animals still faster. The dirt trail quickly turned to mud and it was only the high sides of the road thankfully packed in a precisely built wall of rock on either side that held the mud in place. The horses raced through this muck, kicking up a splatter of mud and small stones. The droning thunder of hooves and the racing of wheels rose above the clamor of falling rain and mounting winds.

Soon Father Jacob gave up hope of finding a village ahead. Recalling the villages behind them, he now sought a place to turn the wagon around. Again and again, his eyes darted to Adrina's still form. A relieved sigh came as he finally reached a spot with an adjacent path where he could turn the four-horse team and wagon around in a tight circle.

Jacob reined the team in and with a pair of leathers in each hand, guided the horses quickly through the twist. A sudden creaking of the wagon's wheels whining above the sound of rain and wind caused him to start. He pulled the reins in the opposite direction. The team turned back, but his reaction came too late. The axle was surely cracked. The left front wheel was out of kilter and it would only be a short time before the wheel broke free.

Jacob shook with dread. Still, he forced himself to think through the situation. Alone he couldn't fix the wheel should it snap. He would have to seek shelter from the storm and attempt to repair the damage later. He didn't move for what seemed a long time. He just sat there, eyes wide, searching. He wanted to see a village along the horizon. The last village they had passed was quite a distance behind them. Perhaps he could reach it if the axle held long enough.

The air around him, which was already cold, grew icy as the storm raged on. Father Jacob wanted to curse, wished his vocation would allow him to curse. To scream aloud just once would have satisfied all his pent up frustration. Instead he found the wisdom of his faith and prayed to Great-Father for guidance. Briefly afterward, the will of the Father flowed strongly through him, but then it was as if the storm sucked away the renewed vitality as readily as rain and wind beat down upon him.

A portent of evil filled his mind like a sickness, yet even in this Jacob attempted to find good. The will of the Father had found him even in this hellish squall. Faith maintained, he continued his scan of the vicinity, his eyes wandering along the adjacent trail while the heavy downpour obscured his vision.

Abruptly he stopped. He squinted, and strained to fix his gaze ahead in the distance where he thought he saw the outline of some low structures. Were they dwellings? Could it truly be? Or was he imagining them?

At a careful gallop, ensuring his pace did not upset the wagon too much, Jacob ushered the four-horse team on. The tiny road was no more than a raised path but it did appear to lead toward a village of sorts. Jacob held his breath with each bump, and prayed the axle would hold, and each time it did, he released it in a heavy sigh.

The mighty structures he envisioned were no more than a collection of thatched huts clumped atop a mound of dirt. But in his mind, Jacob was sure he and Adrina would find warmth inside.

The ailing axle finally gave way with a resonant crack and the wagon slid to an awkward halt. Jacob held Adrina tightly as the wagon toppled to one side. Clinging to his faith, he wiped hopelessness from his face, then picked up Adrina in his arms— Great-Father would not let him fail. He would carry her the remaining distance. Relief was only a few steps away.

The next hundred yards seemed liked miles to Jacob. Step by step, he sloshed through the mud. His back ached and his arms were tired, but he did not stop. A wooden door loomed in the distance and eventually he came to stand before it. He cried out into the stormy sky a solemn thanks to Great-Father, and with a heavy fist he rapped on the door of the hut.

The dull echo of his blows was the only response. In desperation Jacob tried to force the door open but apparently it was barred.

"Go away!" said a meek voice from behind him.

Jacob turned around wearily, his face expressionless as he

looked upon the small boy in front of him. Jacob said, "We need your help."

A middle-aged man appeared from out of the gloom. He approached the boy and put his hand on the boy's shoulder. "You must leave, we cannot help you."

Jacob didn't move.

"Please go, you must go."

"I am Father Jacob, First Minister to the King. I need your help."

"So," said the boy.

The man hushed the boy, and said, "You must go and if you truly be the First Minister to the King, you will know what peril it is to accept strangers during such an evil storm."

And with that, the man took the boy's hand and hurried away.

Chapter Four:
Magic Shield

A trek that would have taken many days by foot would be substantially shortened by wagon. Xith was deeply concerned about getting as far north as quickly as they possibly could. Time was running out. He could sense that now.

Xith looked at the innocence spread out simply on Vilmos' long face and was saddened by it. He wished he could explain to Vilmos the gravity of the situation they were in, how precarious the path ahead was, and how much of it relied on him, a mere boy. Xith only hoped when the time came for Vilmos to act that he would be prepared, that they both would be.

"Beautiful morning!" exclaimed Xith, breaking the silence in the air and casting the shadows from his thoughts.

"What?" asked Vilmos, broken from his own reverie.

"Can't you feel the energy in the air? Don't you just want to draw it in?"

Vilmos sniffed the air. It didn't feel any different from normal.

"Not really," was his quick response.

In and out of his mouth with hearty puffs, Xith began to breathe the moist morning air. Vilmos imagined that Xith was beginning to glow and became entranced by this fanciful notion. Then, subtle changes in skin tone became increasingly apparent until Xith actually did glow. His voice peaking in the middle, Vilmos asked, "Xith, what are you doing?"

Playfulness cascaded away from Xith's eyes. "Sorry," he said after a long pause, "I was going to show you something, but now is not the time. We must wait a while longer."

The road Xith and Vilmos traveled along was arid. The horses' hooves and the wagon's wheels kicked up a large dusty plume, which marked their passage. Ahead in the distance lay a series of rocky hills covered mostly with tall grasses and patched with granite. Beyond, the trail disappeared as it wound through small canyons created by the hills, and beyond the hills was another open flat prairie, with dry tall grasses dancing in the gentle winds traveling lightly across its face. With the slow creaking of the wagon echoing in their ears, they made their way through the hills to the far side of the prairie and beyond.

Vilmos' eyes grew heavy and his yawns became more frequent. His thoughts drifted for a time, unfixed, and eventually settled on images of his mother, whom he missed. A happiness that had been absent for days entered his heart as he pictured her face. His next conscious thought was not until some time later. A sudden shift of the wagon as it hit a large hole in the path thrust him from his sleep.

Caught in the dilemma of how much he could teach Vilmos,

not knowing if the boy was fully ready to begin the lessons, and, if he were, how fast was too fast to progress, Xith tried to reach a decision. It seemed there was time for one last lesson. He must teach it, but was Vilmos ready?

Unable to solve this dilemma, Xith concentrated on the road, which was pockmarked and pitted. He slowed the team down to steady the wagon, and the sluggish pace made the day's progress seem nonexistent. Xith retreated to thoughts of times past and old acquaintances, while Vilmos moved on to let his mind wander, and again enjoyed the passing serenity of the land.

After they had eaten and had rested the horses and were back on the trail moving through a series of wooded knolls and open grasslands, Xith came to a decision. There *was* time for one last lesson. He would teach it as he had planned to.

As the day ended and early night settled in, Vilmos and Xith set up camp in the safety of a clearing within a small woodland oasis. The rather large stand, an oddity this far south, was a hearty growth of fine northern fir, the clipped boughs of which served as an excellent mattress upon which to rest. Lying upon these soft, scented pine boughs, arms crossed and head propped up, tired eyes were allowed a tranquil view, a sedate, star-filled night sky with a gently shining liquid moon.

It was an autumn moon, a moon that was not quite full and loomed low in the sky with the distant, unseen sun casting a cool orange luminescence upon its face. In other times Xith would have called it a blooded moon and the portent would have been one of ominous foreboding, but under the current circumstances it merely moved him into a somber introspective mood.

While he didn't give the omen much thought, he did not cast it away either. Rather, it hung there in the back of his mind while he floated off to sleep and later invaded his few moments of private dreams.

***

Vilmos was the first to wake. Wet droplets of morning dew were the first things to greet him. He didn't want to leave the warmth of his blankets or the soft gentle fir bed to enter the cold uncaring air. A foot, an arm, a leg, slowly probed, and eventually Vilmos slipped from comforts into the cold. As he stood there not moving, adjusting, the only thought in his mind was to find some dry wood. With it, he'd make a fire to take the chill away. After a long gradual coaxing, he set himself to the task.

Xith awoke a short while later to the pleasant crackling sounds of a blazing fire, the warmth of which felt good against his face and hands. He sat up and edged his body closer to the fire, surprised that he hadn't even felt the energy expenditure Vilmos had used to start the healthy blaze with. Perhaps, Xith thought to himself, the boy was ready for the lesson after all.

"Well good morning," Xith said.

Vilmos returned the shaman's warm greeting with one of his own and went in search of the food supplies that had been left in the wagon. He grabbed a little of this and of that, items that appeared most desirable to his sense of smell.

The horses were still loosely tied to a low hanging branch next to the wagon. Thankfully they had not gotten free. Vilmos stroked one of the mares, which was agitated for some reason, until she calmed, then walked back to the fire and sat across from Xith. He offered the shaman a small portion of the carefully selected prizes he had brought back with him. Then he gingerly picked at the food before him, those selections he had not given away to Xith, hard pressed to decide which to eat first because too many arousing scents arose from the stores Misha had prepared.

Vilmos ate a honey cake first, then nibbled on a bit of spiced beef, salted pork and finally a tiny mincemeat pie. He washed it all down with several long swigs from a water bag filled with a sweet drink that tasted of grapes.

When Xith finished, he stood. "Are you ready?" he asked, patting Vilmos on the shoulder, a subdued deviousness was mixed over with half-warm tones.

"Sure," said Vilmos. He stood and crossed to the wagon. He started to climb onto the wagon's running board and stopped abruptly as something hard hit him in the back with a resonant thud.

Vilmos whirled around. "Ouch!"

"You said you were ready." Xith laughed and threw another rock at Vilmos, forcing him to dodge it.

"But you didn't say you were going to throw a rock at me!"

"You should always be prepared for the unexpected. This is the next lesson, our second lesson. You have learned well the forces of fire. Now you shall learn those of air..." so saying, Xith hurled two rocks at Vilmos.

The first Vilmos had expected and dodged successfully, but the second hit him in the back of the hand. Angry, frustrated and not understanding the point Xith was trying to make, Vilmos climbed into the wagon.

"Vilmos, will you ever learn," Xith said. "Here, pick up this rock with your mind." Xith pointed to the small stone in his hand.

"I can't, I don't know how."

"Yes, you do. Midori told me all about your magical pranks. Why do you think I came when I did? I came because I thought you were ready. You have done this before. *Think!*

Xith threw the stone at Vilmos. After waiting a moment, he then picked up another and did the same. Vilmos stood, unmoving and unyielding, not knowing what to do.

"*Stop the rocks from hitting you! Do it now!*" said Xith in a voice that shook Vilmos' mind and stirred his thoughts, but his response was still, "I can't. I don't know how."

"*Think!* It is a very simple process if you have already mastered the forces of levitation. Remember, when you were at home and often you circled things around you? How did you do it? Do you remember?"

"Maybe." Vilmos knew the pranks he had used to drive tutors away, but he didn't understand how it related to a rock being thrown at him.

"Levitation is the process in which you use the element of air to force an object to float. Remember flying, floating above your valley?"

Vilmos' thoughts returned for the first time in a long time to his special place, which he had thought lost, and understood. "That is easy, but I don't—"

"*Hush. Listen!*" Xith said, slipping again into the compelling voice to grab Vilmos' attention. "Instead of using a positive force to lift the object, exert the force out as a wall and repel the object away from you. This is the first lesson, it is the easiest way to repel an object from you. The second lesson is a little trickier and requires a great deal more energy. *Watch!*"

Purposefully sluggish as he overemphasized the strain and the concentration, Xith called the rocks from the ground. One at a time, he slowly lifted the stones and pebbles around them until the air was filled with rocks of all sizes floating through the air. With a summons and a wave of the hand, Xith stirred them to movement as one would a swarm of angry bees. He hurled them through the air, then directed them at himself, where they were reflected harmlessly off an invisible barrier. "Now, do you see?"

"If someone is throwing rocks at you, I guess so."

An immediate pained expression crossed Xith's face, it was clear he was upset. One by one the rocks took flight again, yet this time they were volleyed at Vilmos. Several hit him before he collected his thoughts, his hand hurt, his legs hurt, and he was really getting angry.

It took a stone hitting him square in the face, knocking him to the ground, before he decided this was no longer a game. Vilmos had sudden flashbacks to a barren ridge and raging winds. Vilmos stood and brushed the dust and dirt from his clothes. For a moment, he paid no attention to the debris flying around him.

He collected energy into himself, slowly as Xith had taught him, pulling the energies of creation inside. His only problem was that he didn't know how to properly release it. The energy welled within him until he let it ebb and subside. He cast infuriated eyes upon Xith.

"Continue," Vilmos said simply, haughtily.

Xith smiled an eager smile and slowed the rate of the barrage to a steady, constant attack with fair interval between each wave. "Push them away, Vilmos." Again Xith paused and waited for Vilmos to gather his thoughts. A single pebble at a time, started moving again in slow motion.

One stone was propelling its way toward him. Vilmos pushed out with his energy. It wavered and fell to the ground.

"Yes," Vilmos cried out. He had successfully repelled it. The wall wasn't in place around him, but it was building. His concentration was building as well and so was his confidence.

"Very good," said Xith, "try two."

Two rocks launched at Vilmos at a steady pace. He managed to stop one, but the second one hit him and broke his concentration. He threw his hands up in the air as a sign he wanted to quit. His head ached. He had enough for one day. "Can't we wait till tomorrow?"

"*Try again. You can do it.*" The use of Voice made it mandatory.

As always, Xith's words of praise inspired Vilmos. He knew this time he would not fail. Two stones fell away harmlessly, successfully repelled, but he wasn't prepared for the third that hit him from behind, again on the buttocks.

"Build the wall," Xith said. "Try again."

Especially goaded on by Xith's perky smirk as the last rock had hit him, Vilmos grew angry. He was not going to let Xith or anyone else get the best of him. He stopped one, two, three, four, five and even a sixth stone.

Xith picked up the tempo and changed the directions from which the stones came. Two and three pebbles in groups homed in like beacons on Vilmos from different directions, but again he successfully warded them off.

Sweat dripped off Vilmos' brow. He was tired but Xith would not stop. The air was filled, a clutter of tiny objects, launched at Vilmos. Vilmos cast Xith a lopsided smile, equal to Xith's own menacing grimace. He had built his invisible wall and nothing would get through.

"Nothing will get through," Vilmos whispered to himself. He was nearly exhausted.

Xith did not let up and neither would Vilmos yield though he was past exhaustion and moving toward delirium.

"You waste too much energy, learn to conserve it. *Shape your power*, use it to your advantage."

"I can't do all that at once!" shouted Vilmos, breaking his concentration for an instant.

Xith answered with an increased volley. "*Concentrate!* Do as you did before. Use part of your consciousness toward the task of building the wall and another to shape it. Try to release the spent energy. From this lesson stems the basis for your magical shield, the shield that will protect and keep you in dangerous times. *Now, concentrate!*"

A part of Vilmos digested the words Xith had just spoken while the rest of him set to the task of building the repelling wall. It was so much easier to do before when he had not fully realized what the shaman was trying to teach him through the seemingly simplistic lesson of repelling rocks—*A magical shield, wow!*

Again Vilmos let the wall slip, only for an instant, and was smartly answered with a rock hitting him. The shock cleared his thoughts and jolted his mind into action; again he strove to perform the feat and this time succeeded. He could feel the energy flow within him.

"*Control,* always stay in control. You must control the energy, don't let it control you."

Vilmos had forgotten to exercise control in his momentary lapse. The energy was flowing through him like a tidal wave, flooding his mind. Concentrate, Vilmos thought to himself, I must hold it steady. Gradually, he gripped the energy and regulated it. The power flowed, but did not flood over him.

"Better. Keep it up. Don't lose sight of your center," said Xith.

The assault continued minute after exhausting minute for almost an hour. Xith pushed and pushed until he felt Vilmos had reached his limit, then he purposefully pushed him beyond it.

Vilmos learned fast to control the energy flow and maintain the wall. Soon it became facile, requiring less energy, less thought to maintain. He found his center. He knew exactly how much energy he could build and how to shape it. He was in control. He even thought Xith looked pleased.

An idea came to Vilmos, a plan that seemed easy. Devious thoughts spilled over into this plan. He gathered a small reserve in his energy flow, a slight store inside him. The energy caressed him and Vilmos bathed in it. He split his thinking into three parts, one for the wall, one to keep the flow, and one to begin to conserve the energy for his little scheme.

Vilmos' shield totally fell as he first attempted this feat. Vilmos thought Xith was clearly displeased, but Xith took it as a sign to end the lesson, Vilmos was progressing well.

"No, I want more," Vilmos demanded.

"I think you've had enough for today. You should rest. You have already discovered that from the simple stems the difficult, this is true with all things."

"Just a little more."

Xith waved his hand and began the assault.

A reorganization of his thoughts enabled Vilmos to build a reserve slowly. The wall didn't flicker and he attempted his ploy. Instead of just letting the rocks bounce off his shield, he hurled them away. It took great concentration to keep up all three, the flow, the wall, the casting away, but he managed and now maintained the energy flow, the shield and was successfully repelling the stones.

Xith didn't appear to notice the subtle change and Vilmos was pleased. At first, he could repel only one rock at a time in a given direction, but later with practice he achieved two and then three. He settled there, while he adapted to the strain and soon this too became easy.

Vilmos stared at Xith with a wide grin that Xith didn't even pay attention to. He was certain Xith didn't know what he was up to. He continued until he could deflect an entire barrage at one time and then he went back to throwing them in a few select directions. Although difficult at first, Vilmos succeeded and abruptly he was passing the rocks Xith's way.

Xith was taken completely by surprise. He hadn't even expected such a twist. He was pleased as he allowed the first rock to hit him, very pleased.

"There is hope for you yet. That is a very difficult feat to attempt when just starting," Xith said. He lashed out with his magic and lay to rest all movement around him. "Enough for today. You need to rest. The lesson is ended."

Vilmos was beaming—he had done it. He had surprised the shaman, if only once. Xith fixed Vilmos with a long hard stare, and, without a word, began to harness the horses.

Vilmos climbed onto the wagon's running board, then moved to the seat. He watched as Xith finished harnessing the horses.

"Can I take the reins?" Vilmos asked as Xith climbed into the seat beside him. Xith handed him the leathers. The animals lurched forward under unskilled hands.

"I'm sorry, shaman!" said Vilmos turning to Xith.

"No apology is necessary. You performed excellently."

"Not well, not good, but excellently?" Vilmos' voice crackled in the middle of the last word.

"Yes, you really have! You have learned a great deal more today than I had expected. I had hoped... but then you did. You have learned one of the hardest lessons there is to teach—"

"I did?"

Wordlessly Xith took the reins from Vilmos' hands. "Yes, you have. You have learned to control your energy while your mind is occupied with other tasks, but most importantly you have learned to assimilate your thinking. By grouping the way you think into sections. That is a very great deed in itself.

"It may sound easy, but under duress it is often the hardest thing ever imagined to try. The more you can do at one time the better you will be. If eventually you can do many things without even thinking about them, you will truly be one to be respected.

"You will find the talent very useful. Now maybe you are ready to learn how to control and channel your energy while you sleep. But we will save that lesson for another time."

Xith drove the horses on. For a time the grasslands seemed to spread endlessly before them, then rolling hills returned. As they reached the summit of the last in a long string of green-covered hills, Xith reined in the horses.

"There," Xith said. He reached out with his hand and pointed. "The great sea, West Deep…"

For a few long minutes they sat quietly and stared down at deep blue waters, then Xith coaxed the horses into slow gait. He steered them to a course parallel to the great sea, before whipping at the reins with heavy hands. As he did this, he nervously glanced skyward. The sun was hours past midday.

Chapter Five:
Refusal

Her arms were shaking, weak. Still, she reached out for him and touched him.

A second time you pulled me from the sea, Galan said. She strained to move again, to give Seth back his robe that now covered her. "*What have you done? You must also survive, Seth.*

Seth stretched the tattered robe back over Galan, and covered her face and hands. *I'm no longer sure I want to survive, Galan. Why was I so blind?*

You did not betray your brethren. You could not have known.

But I should have—

—Faith, said Galan. She gripped Seth's hand. *I want to dream, may I see the forest again?*

Never let it dwindle, a voice in Seth's mind repeated, *never let it dwindle, faith will shelter you.* Had Queen Mother known? Seth wondered. And if she had known, why hadn't she tried to stop it?

Seth, said Galan. *Do not dwell on things that cannot be changed. Maybe*

Queen Mother did know and her words were her only way of warning you. It is not wise to try to change fate but there are perhaps ways to alter it slightly.

I did not mean to trouble you with open thought. Seth projected the image—the green of a forest against the backdrop of a white-capped mountain, the sky so blue it was almost purple—into her mind's eye. The idea of such a place's existence truly did seem a wondrous dream to him now.

Confused emotions swept over Seth. Even now he felt the urge to hold Galan as he'd done when he pulled her from the sea.

You may hold me, said Galan, *I feel suddenly cold and empty.*

Waves that had been rolling moderately grew gradually choppier and the open sea became a disquieting place to be. Wind whistled in Seth's ears and the tiny raft began to creak and moan. In the shallow of a trough, where the water on all sides of him filled his field of vision, it seemed as if the sea was opening up to swallow him.

Galan, said Seth. *We must lash ourselves to the raft.*

High seas washed over the raft. Seth strained his mind, and tried to discern a response amongst the tumult. He probed Galan's mind. *Galan? Galan?*

He found only emptiness. Galan was dying.

Their raft was chasing the edge of black clouds now. The scent of rain permeated the air. Soon they would be within the folds of a raging downpour and violent seas. On his hands and knees Seth scrambled toward Galan. He slipped and fell with each movement, and though it was only a short distance, his weakened and weary body was put to the test. Only his near-broken will kept him when endurance and stamina had failed.

Finally at Galan's side, Seth cradled her in his arms. He held her tenderly and firmly, as one might hold a newborn babe if they were afraid it would slip between their fingers. Tears came to his eyes. The moisture burned like fire across his dry eyes. And then, as if in response, bitterly cold rains hit him. Rain, the essence of life—life that abounded with irony while Galan lay dying in his arms.

No my Galan… Do not leave me. I need you— Seth could not finish the sentence. He could not accept the thought of more loss.

No more loss, he promised himself, *no more loss.*

Seth worked to secure Galan to the raft while the storm bludgeoned him with wave after wave that washed the raft's face. Seth vowed that if he and the raft survived the storm so would Galan and only through the sheer force of his will did he maintain his grip.

When he finally got a knot in place, he gasped, and collapsed onto his back. Hungrily, he drank the rain that splashed his face. It seemed a lifetime since he had tasted anything so sweet. Afterward, he worked to lash himself to the raft. This was much easier, though still the work was strenuous. He had to fight the storm and guard against waves that sought to pull him into the sea.

Again, he was left panting. Again he drank as much of the rain as he could force down his burning and swollen throat.

It was then he felt Galan's spirit yearning to be gathered by Great-Father, to be taken home, but he would not let it go, could not let it go. He projected his will into the place her spirit sought to flee, and barred her passage from life. The place between life and death was a cold and empty place just as Galan had warned him it would be.

Right then he vowed he would give his own life before he would allow the last unraveling thread of her life to slip away. In the chaos of his mind, Seth truly believed he could deny death. Any other would not have been able to do what Seth was doing now. Such was the strength of his will and his conviction in his desperation.

He became oblivious to the bludgeoning of the storm. He knew only that he had to hold onto the raft, his precious cargo, and maintain the projection of his will. His thoughts became lost to the internal struggle of his consciousness, his sense of justice over his sense of better judgment. He would not lose the focusing of his will. Barring all else, blocking out sound and sight, Seth escaped reality and slipped further and further into his thoughts, further from what was real and just, while voices filled his mind and his dreams, taking on the role of the just and the unjust.

What is the first law of life, Brother Seth?

Of course the answer is to preserve what Mother-Earth has created so all may enjoy it.

Ahh, yes, but what is the second law of life?

Not to interfere with the natural order of nature and most of all to heed the will of the Father.

Great-Father's word in such matters is final, is it not?

Yes Brother Samyuehl, it is, but the law also says that one is permitted to guide that order or to correct injustices.

To guide or correct yes, but not to interfere with the natural order and that means not to hinder the will of the Father.

When Seth opened his eyes, the world he found was

surprisingly different from the one he had left. The sea was miraculously calm. Night had miraculously arrived and a soft soothing breeze blew upon his skin.

There was picturesque beauty in the face that he looked down upon, even though the eyes were closed and it was gathered in a deathly pale. Vast sadness grew within him, encircling him, and Seth averted his eyes. He peered out into the night sky and time became nonexistent. His only thought amidst mounds of confusion was to maintain his will and keep his vigil. He would not let lose the thread, that last simple thread of life and will.

In and out of consciousness his mind moved, always reaching, always searching, searching for a way to cheat the inevitable, to cheat life and death itself.

Remember, when all seems lost and you cannot find the center of your being, return to that which separates you, distinguishes you, from all else. Return to your thoughts, for they are truly your own. They are you...

Chapter Six:
Crossing

"A curse upon them, Father," Jacob said. He began the long march back to the broken wagon, mud and rain only increased his disillusion, disgust and utter disappointment. His arms and legs were on fire with fatigue, Adrina was a lead weight in his arms that he would not drop.

Jacob staggered and stumbled. He sank to his knees several times, only to return to an uneasy stagger moments afterward. Mud covered his cloak, his arms and even his face.

He began to chuckle to himself as an increased downpour ironically washed the muck away. A few more steps, he promised himself, not realizing he didn't know what he would do when he did reach the wagon. *Faith,* whispered a tiny voice in his mind, *faith everlasting...*

"F-a-ther!" crackled a distant voice, softly intermixed with the sound of the storm.

At first Jacob thought it was the voice of his conscience

speaking to him again, but then the call repeated. He stumbled and turned back toward the huts. As he did this he fell to his knees and, still clutching the princess tightly, he looked up to see an ancient man with a long, white beard standing in an open doorway.

"Quickly, now!" the man hissed.

Finding renewed vigor, Jacob did as the old man bade. Rain beating down upon him washed away the mud from his most recent fall by the time he reached the doorway.

"I won't forget this Father! I will never forget this," Jacob called out to the sullen sky. He revoked his ill-spoken curse.

Quickly Father Jacob slipped off the princess' soaked jacket and the wet clothes beneath which were drenched both from rain and perspiration from a renewed fever. After throwing the wet things unceremoniously into a pile on the floor, he laid Adrina onto the bed that the kindly man indicated. Immediately, he pulled its thick blankets tightly around her pale, limp body.

"Get me some moist towels," Jacob demanded of the old man.

Directly the man returned with clean cloths and a bowl of cool water. He joined Father Jacob at the bedside. "Here, let me do that for you. You are tired, you must rest. I am Master T'aver and I gather that you are Father Jacob. I am sorry about before, but you must know of the superstitions of my people. I take great risk allowing you into my home on a night such as this. Can you not feel the malice of the storm?"

Jacob heard little of what the other told him. It wasn't that he was ungrateful, but his attentions were on Adrina and he cared for nothing else. He wet a cloth in the bowl, rung it out and placed it on Adrina's forehead. The increasing fever magnified his worries and he bent his head in solemn prayer. He needed guidance. He prayed for strength and continued faith.

To Jacob it seemed hours later that he raised his head and whispered, "I am ready," to the fading echoes of voices in his mind.

He cleared his mind and set to the task ahead. Somehow, wisdom came easily to his thoughts. Power flowed through his mind and center. His will became centralized, focused, and this time there was no block between the power of his mind and his heart. He began the litany of healing and life, yet this time the song-prayer was different from the one that he had tapped into before. It was animate and latent with power.

His words departed from those of the Kingdom spilling slowly over into those of another time, becoming for a time a blend of present and past, and then finally focusing on the old tongue.

It was an odd sensation to feel within himself the will of Mother-Earth so potent—few males had ever been granted such a gift from the Mother. Perspiration flowed down his brow and dripped from the tip of his nose to touch the floor below with a splash in the small pool forming beneath the spot where he stood, engrossed in a litany of words so ancient they glistened with subtle hints of power. But it was not so much the words Jacob spoke that created the power, rather the delicate focusing they created in his mind to gather his will and direct it precisely.

Over the course of the hours that ensued, Father Jacob maintained the chanting rhythm and the healing began. Minutes became hours and hours unfolded one by one. The power of life flowed from Jacob's words and took new form inside the young princess, whose face was still wrapped in a pale, deathlike mask, and as that strength flowed between them, Jacob could feel hours of his life slip accordingly away.

Utter exhaustion played out on his features and when he was finally forced to quit due to his fatigue, Jacob slumped over at the side of the bed. He rested his head on soft covers, arms raised and crossed over his knees. He was trembling and there were tears in his eyes. He knew he had succeeded. Already he could sense the fever lifting from Adrina.

But what had it cost him, he asked himself. They were miles away from Castle Fraddylwicke, miles away from the sea, and so very far away from Alderan. Soon exhaustion forced sleep upon him and Father Jacob fell fast asleep.

**

"Good Father Jacob, can you hear me?" a soft voice called out. "The dawn has come and gone, and still you sleep…"

Jacob stirred. He heard the unpleasant sounds of hammering now, which suddenly sounded to him as if someone was driving a spike into his head. Still half in a daze, he opened his eyes. He looked about the room. He was lying supine on a cot opposite the hut's only bed. His eyes flashed with surprise as he realized the bed was empty. "Where is Princess Adrina? Have you done something to her?"

The old man batted his eyes at Father Jacob as if the priest had just stung him. "That one is full of wind and fire. She's been directing my sons' efforts all this morning, fixing the wheel on that wagon of yours."

Jacob moved sluggishly to a sitting position. "And you are?"

"I am Master T'aver," said the old man. He scratched his long white beard. "You came upon my home during the devil's own squall yester eve. You truly are First Minister to the King. You performed a miracle last night that never in all my years have I seen."

Jacob cocked his head and looked out the window. "The banging has stopped."

"Yes, it is near midmorning. Some hours now my sons have labored at that wheel. It must be fixed. You should eat now and with godspeed you'll be on your way."

Jacob started to stand, T'aver put a halting hand to his shoulder. "Wait. The food will come. We should first talk. There are things you must know if you are to continue your journey."

"What can *you* possible know of my journey?" Jacob asked. Again he moved to stand. The fog in his mind was clearing now. He was worried about the young princess. He hadn't expected a full recovery and Adrina was just strong-minded enough to be out and about while still very ill.

T'aver moved a chair to Jacob's cot. "Five days after the last full moon, I received a portentous message from an old friend. The message was in the form of a scroll, sealed magically—"

Jacob's eyes went wide at the mention of the forbidden craft— it was one thing to use prayers and gifts from Father and Mother, quite another to tap into the fabric of the world.

Master T'aver continued, "And meant only for my eyes. It told me things I didn't want to believe—not that I doubted the word of the Watcher."

Again Jacob's eyes grew wide with astonishment.

"But I truly did not believe until your arrival yester eve… Trust the girl's instincts Father Jacob. She walks under a charm…" T'aver seemed about to say something more, but just then the door opened and an old woman carrying a tray of food entered the hut. Master T'aver bade Jacob eat and said no more.

***

The four-horse team seemed strangely unresponsive as Father Jacob directed it back to the main thruway. Above, the sky was clear and deep blue. While Adrina was hopeful it would remain that way, she couldn't deny the ill feeling building up from within. She cast Father Jacob a concerned glance and wondered at his silence. He had said little to her since awaking and nothing of his conversation with T'aver.

At a quiet, unbroken pace the journey continued, with the musty and pungent odor of the swamp eventually replaced by a fresh, cool breeze that promised of the coast and the sea ahead. Adrina watched Jacob guide the wagon repeatedly, chiding the horses to swifter and swifter speeds. She was sure they would arrive in Alderan too late to stop whatever was taking place. She was also sure Father Jacob felt the same thing.

That night they camped only when it became too hazardous to continue along the shrouded road. Adrina slept bundled in many blankets in the back of the wagon. Jacob slept on the ground beside a meager fire.

Adrina came awake before dawn and, as the false dawn gathered, Father Jacob and Adrina began their race again. Soon the sea came into view and a wonderful sensory explosion of salt air and sea life followed. In the distance, seagulls speckled the air and dotted the landscape of a rocky coastline, their calls reaching the approaching two on gentle breezes.

Adrina's face flushed with sudden color, turning from the ashen pale it had held to a rosy alabaster as sea breezes blew against her cheeks. A smile touched her lips and she touched her hand to Jacob's and momentarily held it tight. The sun and the breeze felt good. For a brief moment, she thought of Lady Isador. Lady Isador who longed for southern breezes and tall grasses.

"I made it to the sea," said Adrina glumly, her voice so soft and shallow that it blended into and was lost in the sounds of wind rushing past her ears and birds in the sky overhead. Her eyes fixed on a point out along the horizon and out across the waters of the sea ahead. Somewhere out there was Prince William. Adrina was sure of that now. She saw his blue, blue eyes staring up at her again.

Adrina prepared herself to ask Father Jacob a question that had been in the back of her mind for some time. She was already sure what Jacob's answer would be, but felt she had to ask anyway. Either Jacob would confirm her fears or—and this is the reason Adrina felt compelled to speak—he would tell her that things were not as bad as they seemed. She took in a deep breath, laced her fingers together and then spoke. "Father Jacob…"

Jacob cast her a sidelong glance.

"Do you believe King Jarom would try to kill my brother?" There, she said it, but she didn't feel any better for the saying. She took another deep breath and braced herself for Jacob's response.

Jacob seemed to sense her anguish. He put the reins for the team in one hand and with his free hand touched hers. "That is a question I have asked myself again and again, but I told myself I did not want to answer. The fact is that King Jarom murdered King Charles and that obviously he wants to stop Prince William from reaching the North to bring word of this terrible deed to King Andrew."

"What could King Jarom possibly have gained from killing Charles?"

"It could be that he wishes to restore Vostok to its former glory."

Adrina's eyes widened. She recalled something Keeper Martin had told her before they had entered the swamps. "If King Jarom took Sever, what would be next? Would he go beyond the disputed lands?"

Jacob's mouth dropped open. Adrina had never seen him at a loss. It was clear he hadn't considered this.

"King Jarom may lust for power," Jacob said, "but invasion is another thing altogether. It would mean plunging the kingdoms into an all-out war. As it is now, what he has done may already mean war, but that would depend on the evidence Prince William brings to King Andrew and the decision of the Alliance."

"The lady in the forest told me that King Jarom sees himself seated on Imtal's throne. Was Vostok once that vast?"

"Never that vast, but at the end of the Race Wars, when only the five sons of the Alder remained in power, King Jarom the First controlled nearly all the lands from Neadde to Ispeth. It was his Blood Soldiers that pushed the enemy back to the sea near the mouth of the Opyl River, and it was he with his own bare hands that committed patricide and started the last Great War."

Adrina felt suddenly sick and sorry she had spoken at all. She said nothing more, and neither did Father Jacob.

Upon reaching the rocky coast, Father Jacob turned the wagon in a wide semi-circle and took the southerly route. Alderan was now only a half-day's ride away. With luck, they would reach the city before dusk. Another question neither Adrina nor Jacob wanted to answer was whether this would be too late to stop what was already set in motion.

***

The section of the coastline they traveled along became a series of rocky crags with sharp, jutting spurts that jumped out into the yearning sea. Rough-hewn, carved by the forces of nature that acted upon the waters and enveloped them at times, they seemed somehow alive.

The wind, a steady gale with mixed patches of warm and cool, often carried with it a soft salty spray as waves crashed into the shore, and as the afternoon sun gathered itself full in the sky the day still held the promise of clear, cloudless skies.

Adrina sat silently, her hands clasped tightly together. She reflected on earlier thoughts, letting her gaze wander as the wagon twisted and turned.

The breezes became cooler as the sun began to settle toward the glossy blue waters of the sea, and the cool air felt good against Adrina's skin. Still, Father Jacob stopped the wagon for a moment to retrieve two blankets from the rear. He searched through the satchels of foodstuffs and came up with a rounded loaf of black bread and a dark yellow cheese.

The meal was a hurried affair. Soon after finishing, Father

Jacob drove the horses onward. It was a quick start, followed by an unwholesome lull that hung in the air. Even the sea breezes seemed to be aware of it as they softened. Then the pleasant sounds of the great West Deep disappeared altogether. The calls of the gulls died out. The splashing of the waves became subdued. Even the rolling of the wagon's wheels became secondary to the great quiet that was all around them.

Father Jacob slowed the horses to a sedate pace. His eyes searched. Adrina remained silent, her thoughts mostly idle and insubstantial now, though she could not shake the voice of the lady from her mind. It unnerved her. It called out to her and the fact that it grew stronger the farther along the coast they rode did not make her feel any easier.

A sudden change in the air around them came as a single, dark cloud passed in front of the sun, momentarily creating an eerie shadow across the land. With the momentary darkness came a spontaneous downward shift in temperature. Jacob and Adrina clutched the woolen blankets more tightly and subconsciously shivered to ease the sudden chill.

The horses cast frightened whinnies into the air, their sixth sense warning that danger lurked near. Adrina's heart seemed to stop beating in a temporary lapse until the sun's brightness and warmth once more covered her. Yet even with the warmth's return, the chill was not so readily cast away. Rather it lingered much, much longer. It was as if an evil hand reached out and stroked her, telling her, bragging to her, that it was near.

Adrina cast a glance heavenward. The sky was as clear as it had been a short while ago. The dark cloud was gone, vanished, as if it had simply evaporated after it had passed. As her eyes returned to the horizon, she grasped Jacob's hand and pointed to an object far in the distance. Jacob followed the direction her outstretched hand led, out along the coast and into the dark waters. However, what Adrina directed him to was not out amidst the darkening waters, but across them, back along the serpentine coastline. A cloud of dust arose and, it seemed a large group of riders rapidly approached.

"Father Jacob," said Adrina, "I don't have a good feeling about this."

Father Jacob seemed to still be shaking off the previous chill. He made a quick scan of the area, apparently looking for a place to hide, before he replied, "Rocks and squat grasses don't offer much cover, child. This wagon is too slow and awkward to maneuver in this rough terrain…"

Jacob paused in thought, Adrina cut in, "Perhaps, we could unhook the team and proceed on horseback."

"By the time we did that it would already be too late…" As he spoke, it seemed an idea came to Jacob. He had Adrina pull her long black hair back and tie it up in her scarf. Afterward he pulled the blanket around her so that it partially concealed her face and then he did likewise. The air was chilly and it wouldn't have been all that unusual for them to be bundled against the cold and the spray from the sea.

Jacob didn't stop the horses as he had thought to do, but instead proceeded at a slow pace. The riders steadily approached. Adrina's gaze grew gradually downcast until she was practically staring only at the dirt in front of her. The riders slowed as they passed for a cursory inspection, but quickly increased their pace and sped away.

Not raising her downward gaze, Adrina saw only the riders' mounts, a blur of hindquarters and forelegs, as they passed. She closed her eyes and nearly fell asleep until Jacob nudged her to tell her everything was all right.

Adrina lowered the blanket, but still kept it about her shoulders. The danger was gone, or so it seemed. She cast a nervous glance over her shoulder at the group of riders and then watched as Father Jacob flicked the reins to hasten the team.

They continued to wind their way along the serpentine coast, and Adrina cast her fears away. The trail became steadily rock-strewn, making passage over it rough and often very difficult. Large boulders that had to be circumnavigated sprang up in the middle of the trail and the width of the coastal road became steadily narrower.

Adrina followed and wandered among the empty waters breaking the coastline with her eyes, searching for that which was not there. The voice in her mind had grown sullen and quiet, and now her thoughts wandered free with the waves, rolling and sinking with each as they turned under, rising as each new wave was born, racing as they crashed into the rocky shore.

The emptiness was still present, however, and the sounds of life still void. This lifelessness played heavily on Adrina's thoughts. With each new curve, she wondered what lay on the other side. The coastal highway they rode along wasn't usually a bustling thoroughfare so she didn't think it was odd not to see any other passers by. It wasn't that she really wanted to see any, actually, but she wouldn't have minded seeing a friendly face—she didn't consider Jacob's pensive stare friendly or comforting.

Her thoughts slowly turned to the encroaching night. The sky was still clear but Father Jacob had told her storms here usually came suddenly and frequently.

Adrina cocked her head and listened to a sound carried by the wind. "Father Jacob?" asked Adrina with a timid voice. "What is that?"

"What is what?"

"Can't you hear it?" Adrina asked.

Jacob pulled the reins taut and the horses slowed to a steady halt. "Can I hear what?"

"The singing."

"Singing?" Jacob tossed her an odd glance then put his hand to her forehead. "Stick out your tongue child?"

"Father Jacob, listen…"

A puzzled frown crossed Jacob's lips. "Maybe I do hear something, then again it doesn't sound like sing—" A distant low rumbling came from behind them now. "It is only thunder, child."

It took both a moment to realize that the thunder they heard was hooves against the rocky ground. Frantically they spun around and stared back down the trail behind them. A clump of dots trailing dust slowly became visible—the band of riders was returning.

"Still, that's not what I hear, Father Jacob," Adrina said.

"Wait a min—" Jacob gasped. "By the Father, I do hear something."

Adrina grabbed the reins from Jacob's lap and whipped them.

The horses took off at a gallop, causing the wagon to jolt wildly. Adrina glanced behind them. She could make out single objects now, horses and riders. The group was gaining on them. "They'll catch us before we can get away," she said.

Apparently feeling suddenly inspired, Jacob shouted, "Give me the reins, child! We'll give them a run for it!"

Adrina didn't give Jacob the reins, the strong presence of evil had returned. She didn't know whether it was from behind her or ahead, but she knew it was there. She strained her tired eyes, trying to see what was ahead in the distance. A small sandy inlet settled where the ridgeline sloped down to the sea, forming a cove of sorts. This was the first place she'd seen where the road ran directly along the waters. The section appeared to have been washed away by the recent heavy rains and the inlet thus formed.

"There!" she shouted. Adrina didn't have to point to the object in the sand now, she knew Jacob saw it too.

"Halt!" sounded a loud, masculine voice that appeared drastically close.

Both Adrina and Jacob skewed their eyes left to see a rider that seemed to suddenly appear beside them. As a reflex Adrina halted the wagon. Her mind was filled with sudden panic. Why now when they were so close? She wanted to cry. Her eyes swelled with tears that slowly began to roll down her cheeks.

"Father, why?" she sobbed raising her voice aloft, not really asking Jacob and not really asking Great-Father, rather addressing them both.

The face that loomed over her, angry and fierce, seemed to lunge at her as it stepped from the horse to the wagon's deck. Just as the man reached his hands out to grab Adrina, Jacob snatched the reins from Adrina's hands and whipped them as hard as he could.

"Go away, leave us alone!" shouted Adrina.

The four horses dashed responsively forward and the rider, who had been struggling to maintain his balance as the wagon sprang forward, tumbled to the ground. A crunching sound an instant later said he struck the hard ground fatally. Adrina regained the reins from Father Jacob and a chase commenced with Adrina's only goal being the sandy inlet not far ahead. She was certain something was there, but exactly what she didn't know.

"I don't believe it!" shouted Jacob, "Look, there is another group of them ahead of us... Give me the reins back... We can't outdistance them, we have to think through this logically."

"No," shrieked Adrina. She slapped Jacob's hands away.

The wagon shook and rattled as it raced along the rough trail. Heedless, Adrina urged the horses on until the back end of the wagon was bouncing into the air. Jacob tossed nervous glances behind. It was clear he was more concerned about those that loomed up from behind than those that were ahead of them. The riders behind them were chasing them while, from what Adrina could see of the group ahead, they weren't moving at all.

"What are they waiting for?"

"I wish I knew," Jacob said. "Wait a minute, are those Kingdom standards?"

"So what if they are."

Jacob stared long. "Great-Father, they are! It must be the column. We're safe, Adrina, we're safe."

Those were Jacob's last words as a mailed hand cuffed him. His head struck the wagon's deck below Adrina's feet with a crunch that sent chills up Adrina's back. Her terror-filled shriek was cut short as she fought off hands that sought to grab the reins from her. Panic gripped her mind. Her screams became wild and shrill. Suddenly, strong hands snatched the reins away from her and the wagon was brought to an abrupt halt.

The same strong hands twisted Adrina and wrenched her from the wagon's seat, throwing her roughly to the ground. Momentarily everything went black as the wind was knocked out of her. Adrina scrambled backwards on the ground as the angry man swept down upon her. He picked her up again a moment later and began to shake her violently. Adrina's head bobbed and her teeth rattled. Her thoughts stifled by fright. Even when the man stopped shaking her, still she trembled uncontrollably.

"Treacherous murderer!" shouted the angry voice of the man whose strong hands squeezed into Adrina's shoulders with increasing vigor.

Frustration and despair lead Adrina to tears, but anger and pain soon took over. She clawed and kicked her captor, raking him across the face.

With one hand the large man roughly pulled back her long hair as she struggled to break free, while his other hand groped for something, Adrina didn't know what. Then out of the corner of her eye, she caught a glint of something shiny. She swallowed a heart-sized lump in her throat as a short, fine blade was applied to her upturned neck.

"A-dri-na?" came a distant voice.

Upon hearing her name, the terror-filled fog in Adrina's mind cleared. "Let me go, let me go," she screamed.

"Adrina?"

Adrina stopped kicking and clawing her captor. She turned. The first face she saw was familiar to her. "Emel!" she cried. She wiped the tears from her face, and reached her hands out to embrace him. Still, she shook uncontrollably. "But you were... that was... you then... Where is my brother? Has he already reached Alderan? Is it too late to stop him?"

The large dark-skinned southerner holding Adrina did not let her go. Instead he returned the blade to her throat. "By the Father, her blood *will* stain this blade."

"Hush. Let her go, what are you doing you fool?"

"But they killed Wrennyl!" The Southerner spun Adrina around and stared at her.

Adrina saw fury in his eyes. "It was a mistake, a mistake. We didn't know who you were and it was an accident that... that... he... fell, an accident."

Emel snatched Adrina away from the angry man. His free hand went to his sword in its sheath. "I said, back off, back off..."

Menacingly the large Southerner took a step toward Adrina. His blade poised ready to strike, he spoke, "Lord Valam will surely hear off this... Wrennyl was a good man!"

"I trust he will," said Emel, "especially since this is the Princess Adrina."

The man turned pale. "*The* Princess Adrina?"

"Yes, the Princess Adrina."

The Southerner began babbling an apology. "I'm sorry, Your

Highness. You must forgive me. I didn't know… I didn't know, I swear it."

The man was sniveling and in tears, but Adrina said nothing. Her shoulders ached where he had gripped them and she just now got her shivers under control. She wiped tears from her cheeks, and turned away as the man sank to his knees.

"By Great-Father," moaned Emel in a low tone, "say something to him please. If they think you took offense, he'll get lashes. He is a family man. Do you know what that'll mean to him."

Adrina just then noticed the press of riders around her. "Lashes?" she asked.

"Say it now, please!"

Adrina turned back to the man. "Rise please, stand true. I accept your apology. Though in the future, I would ask that you treat a lady as a lady should be treated."

The Southerner stood and straightened his hunched posture. Evident relief passed over his face moments later.

Sadness and relief triggered something in Adrina. She looked around wildly, then started running. "Emel, come quickly!" she called back over her shoulder, "Come quickly, it is Prince William!"

There was a low moaning from behind them now as the two raced away. Uneasily, Father Jacob settled back onto the seat of the wagon, a hand raised to his cheek. Several riders quickly came to his aid and helped him down from the wagon.

***

A single figure lay washed onto the beach, folded into the area where the recent storms had formed a sandy hollow. Wreckage lay scattered on the shore around him. Adrina ran to him. She knelt in the wet sand beside him, and touched a hand to his cheek. She expected him to greet her with his warm blue eyes, but, to her horror and shock, his skin was cold, cold and stiff with death.

"He is dead," Adrina said, "we are too late... Alderan? How far are we from Alderan?" Adrina grabbed Emel about the shoulders. "Where is Prince Valam?"

"Our party from Quashan' circled north around Alderan only a few hours ago. We expected to meet the column on the north side of the city, but we found nothing. His Highness sent our detachment north and another east to find the encampment. His aim was to proceed to the city outpost. Why aren't you with the column? Did something happen?"

Adrina explained as best she could what happened after Emel had left the column.

Emel swept Adrina up in his arms. Caught up in the reassurance of his touch and the warmth of his embrace, Adrina pressed her lips against Emel's. For a moment, Emel returned the passion of her kiss, then he stood stiffly and turned away from her.

"No doubt Captain Trendmore is our traitor," Emel said, "and more likely than not, he ordered the column to turn north at the sea instead of south. I never should have left you... This is all my fault. I didn't listen to what the lady said and look what has happened."

"It wasn't your fault, Em—"

"What about my father's accident?"

"Emel, I don't think you could've stopped it even if you had been there. Now is not the time to dwell on the could have beens."

"Indeed," said a voice from behind Adrina. Startled, she turned to see a strange small man and a boy. They were seated in the shaded part of the rocks behind her, and she had not seen either before.

Emel immediately drew his blade and stepped between Adrina and the stranger. "Proceed with caution friend, I'd just as soon run you through as not. What are you doing here?"

"Same as you," said a strange short man as he stood. "We were drawn here."

"Stay where you are," warned Emel.

The stranger took a step toward Emel. His hands were raised, and it seemed to Adrina he was unarmed. "Here is where the paths cross. The many become one for a short time," so saying, the man reached out his hand to Emel.

Emel lunged forward, his blade arched high, then it plunged deep into the man's side. Adrina's scream came too late.

Chapter Seven:
Alderan

Vilmos stepped protectively across Xith's prone form and waited for the assailant to make his next move. He was angry and magic raged unchecked through him.

"We are friends, not enemies," Vilmos said. "I don't want to have to kill you."

The man raised his sword defensively. Vilmos felt himself losing control of the magic.

"Put away your weapon," Vilmos said. "Please."

"Emel!" yelled the man's companion.

"Stay out of this, Adrina. I will let no one harm you." Emel turned back to Vilmos. "Tell your companion to get up none too quickly. Or I'll run him through again."

"*Trust* is a two-way path. *Put away* your *weapon*," said Xith, using the Voice to calm. Then he grabbed Vilmos' hand and said, "*Control!* Remember that anger and that hatred for another time..."

Xith gasped for breath. "The stones... in my bag, you'll find...

a sack with five stones, bring… it to me…"

Vilmos brought the small bag of stones, but never looked away from the one who had attacked Xith.

"You are… swift… with a blade," Xith said through gasps, "we may soon… have need… of your skills."

Voices called out from the road now, "Emel, are you all right? We heard shouting?… Emel, do you need help?"

"*Answer* them. Tell them you are fine. *Tell them you will be along presently…*

"We are fine," Emel shouted. "We will be along presently."

"There isn't much time. Gather round, gather round. You too, young princess—" Xith winced from pain. "—Vilmos, the stones."

"Are you dying?" Vilmos asked with the utmost seriousness.

"Your apprenticeship is hardly at an end. He barely grazed my side." Vilmos looked down at the shaman's saturated robe. "Even small wounds bleed and the pain is not in my side, it is in my head. Our friend there has had quite a trial. I shouldn't have attempted to connect to his mind without blocking the flow of feelings. Never have I been so overwhelmed by anything…"

Xith winced again. "But I needed to find out what he knew. Just as I needed to know about you, Princess Adrina."

"Then you heard everything we said before?" Adrina asked.

Vilmos turned to regard the young woman. Before his thoughts had been on other things, he hadn't really noticed her until now. Momentarily he was caught up in her great brown eyes.

"Seated there in the shadows, it was hard not to. Do not worry, your secrets are safe with me. As I said, and as my companion, Vilmos, said, we are friends. We were drawn to this place for a reason. Each of us has a part in changing the many paths, for here the paths converge."

"How do we know we can trust you?" Emel asked.

Adrina asked, "And what of Prince William? Is that him?"

"Emel Brodstson, even the lady of the night knew the way of your heart."

Emel's face flushed red.

"And no," Xith said turning to Adrina, "that is not Prince William… If I probed correctly, our friend's name is Seth. He traveled here across the West Deep from a place called East Reach… They were ambushed and only a few survived. In the end, only two.

"The rest of his memory was rather disjointed, but as the other there is human and he isn't, I can only assume that some sort of struggle took place on this very beach, and here he lost his only other companion. We will know more when he regains consciousness, but for now we have more important things to concern ourselves with."

"What do you mean not human?" Emel exclaimed.

Adrina put her hand on Emel's shoulder, but he brushed it away. Xith said nothing. He only stared.

"By the Father, it is you!" called out a voice from behind them. Vilmos turned to see an aged man dressed in a dirty black robe. One side of the man's face was swollen and bruised. "How long has it been, ten… no twelve years." The man's expression became sullen. "Returned from under-mountain just as you said. I didn't want to believe it when I heard it yesterday morning."

Xith regarded the elder for a moment, then said, "You, Jacob do not look well, and I'd heard you were now King's First Minister... And it is nearly thirteen."

Jacob said, "I should have known I'd find you at the heart of all this."

Xith smiled now, apparently at the other's expense. "I am merely one of the fools on the board. I hope I know my part and move accordingly."

"Father Jacob, you know him?" asked Adrina.

"Of course I know the..." Xith put a silencing hand to his lips and Jacob spoke no more.

"Do you wish to inquire about my lineage now?" asked Xith of Emel who still had his sword drawn, "Or do you wish to know of the fall of Alderan?"

Princess Adrina's eyes went wide. She turned to Emel and glared at him. "Fall?" she asked.

Father Jacob waved Emel's weapon away. Emel sheathed the sword then said, "All is well in Alderan."

"All *appears* well in Alderan, because that is what was meant. Do we argue now, or do we ride for Alderan?"

"We ride."

"Yes, we ride!"

"To Alderan," whispered Adrina.

***

The group waited in the forested hills to the east of Alderan. Father Jacob sat beside Xith, "Yes, we will listen," he said.

Vilmos, Emel and Adrina sat likewise. They formed a loose circle around the shaman.

Xith cleared his throat, turned his eyes around the circle, then said, "The Alliance of Kingdoms is all but broken. King Jarom has been flooding the upper southlands with men loyal to his cause for many months. And where he doesn't have soldiers, he has spies. His spies are everywhere and his reach is long…"

Father Jacob and Adrina nodded fast agreement.

Xith continued. "In all but name, Jarom *is* the absolute ruler of the four kingdoms of the south. Only King Charles was brave enough to oppose him, and while this was true up until a few short weeks ago, it is no longer true. The Kingdom of Sever is now without king and its heir, its heir—"

Adrina interrupted, "What of my brother?"

"King Jarom fully expected King Andrew to answer King Charles' call for aid and for the safekeeping of Charles' son, Prince William. He may be quite surprised to find only a prince, but then again, Prince Valam's death—" Adrina's face flushed white. She began to tremble and Xith expected her to say something or to burst into tears, but she didn't. "—will allow him to usurp *all* lands south of the Trollbridge, all the lands of the South. Already troops march on Quashan'. With the cities' commander gone and the garrison sent north, the city will easily fall."

"I was just in Quashan'," Emel said. "The whole of the garrison was in company."

Xith turned frank eyes on the untrusting young guardsman. "If King Jarom can pay off a Chief-Captain of Imtal Garrison right under the king's nose, surely he can likewise persuade a Quashan' garrison commander or one of his captain's or even one of his under-captains to relay an incorrect order."

"But what can we do?" asked Father Jacob. "A great force must have laid siege to Alderan. We have no more than forty riders."

"Fifty six," Emel said.

Princess Adrina's downtrodden expression turned upward briefly.

"I suspect Alderan was taken without a fight from the inside," Xith said. "For all we know, they marched straight into the city under Kingdom standards and the citizens greeted them openly."

Xith took a long swig from a water bag. His throat was dry and overworked. The ride to Alderan had gone smoothly, but not quietly. "Once Prince Valam is dealt with, the forces in the city will turn their sights on joining the march on Quashan'. This is what we *must* count on…"

***

"Are your men ready?" Xith asked.

Emel nodded. Xith joined Father Jacob deeper in the midst of the trees and there the two spoke in hushed tones.

Fifty-six ridesmen anxiously waited near the edge of the forest for the dusk shadows to deepen. They had been waiting in the trees for several hours now.

Adrina scratched absently at the mosquito bites on her arms, hands and face. The City of Alderan seemed deceptively quiet. Emel's closeness to her was reassuring, but she was still ill at ease. She glanced to the strange wise man that had told her to stop calling him Watcher. "My name is Xith," he had told her.

The conversations with Xith had left Adrina filled with dread. Especially his seemingly casualness about that fact that Prince Valam would most probably be dead when and if they found him. Adrina hadn't burst into tears then, though it had taken considerable effort not to. Now she could only remember fond thoughts of her only brother—big as a bear and with a heart twice any normal man's. It was in Valam's shadow that she used to walk the streets of Imtal and his dreams of seeing all of the world that filled her young mind with thoughts of fantastic adventures.

"Are you all right?" whispered Emel in Adrina's ear.

Adrina nodded.

"Good. You and Father Jacob will wait here until we return. If we're not back by sunup, leave. Make progress north as fast as you—"

Adrina cut Emel off with a hiss. "I'll not stay here and worry through the night. Where you go, I go. Remember the words of the lady?"

"Only death awaits in Alderan," returned Emel.

Adrina glared at him. "You expect me to turn away when every hand counts? I am as good with a blade as you are, perhaps better."

"Besting me on the practice field is not the same thing, Adrina," Emel said coldly.

Xith returned. "Keep your voices to a whisper," he said.

Adrina started to speak. Xith raised a silencing hand. He wavered his gaze, his eyes shining as he stared out into the darkening land. "Everyone back and stay down," he said, "not a sound anyone…"

Soon figures carrying shielded lanterns appeared from the dark shroud. Behind them came horses and riders. Behind the riders, heavily laden wagons. Behind the wagons, more horses, more men. From her vantage point, Adrina began counting them as they passed. She stopped as the numbers swelled to over two hundred.

ၵၙ The Kingdoms & The Elves ၵၙ

Adrina found it unsettling that she heard only the occasional squeaking of wagon wheels to mark the group's passage. Riders were leading their mounts whose hooves were apparently padded. The weapons and armor of the soldiers she saw were also apparently padded, for as they passed, the normal clink-clink of metal scraping metal was absent. The group was traveling southeast, southeast to Quashan' just as Xith had said they would.

The southeastward passage continued for more than an hour, and then for an hour afterward, nothing. No shielded lights pierced the darkness and no sounds pierced the uncanny silence.

Out of the corner of her eye, Adrina saw Xith raise his hand and suddenly the press of bodies around her was absent. The small band of Kingdom ridesmen were suddenly sweeping toward Alderan City. Split into three tiny groups, they would strike the city from the north, east and south. The intent was to make the enemy remaining in the city think they were under attack by a large force. Adrina didn't know exactly what Xith hoped to accomplish by this, for surely the defenders would discover very quickly that only a few dozen men were carrying out the attack.

Adrina felt a hand on her shoulder. She spun around, surprised to find it was Emel. She stared at him in momentary disbelief. "You didn't go with the others?"

"Xith asked that I remain, and I have." Emel didn't seem happy about the prospect, but Adrina was—Emel wouldn't die with the others.

Adrina's smile died when she saw Xith's glowing eyes upon her.

"Vilmos, Adrina and Emel you'll ride into the city with me," Xith said, in a quiet voice. "Only Father Jacob is to remain behind.

He'll watch our new companion, and he knows what to do should we not return. To your mounts! Our route into the city should be wide open soon. Hurry now, there is no time to waste..."

The Kingdom ridesmen attacked the city from three directions. Xith, Adrina, Emel and Vilmos made their way to the city from the south. Adrina was surprised to hear the sounds of a raging battle coming from the northern sectors of the city now. One thing she had neglected to consider, as Emel had pointed out, was that Alderan was a Kingdom city and had been a united city even before there had been a Kingdom. Apparently those in the city thought the King's army had come to liberate them. No true Kingdomer would sit idly if they thought the King's army was storming the city.

Under this shroud of confusion, the four crept into Alderan. After they had safely passed the city gates, Xith signaled for them to stop and gather round.

"We make for the city center." Xith spoke very softly. "Even now all routes to the keep will be guarded. If for some reason anyone is separated, watch your way with care, but head for the keep at once. Remember, all through streets are set up like the spoke of a wheel. They all lead to the center hub, and the keep."

Xith paused, then looked to Adrina. "To get into and around the inner keep unseen, we'll need your help."

Adrina stared blankly at Xith.

Speaking for Adrina, Emel said, "She's never been to Alderan."

"Down to the last detail, Imtal Palace was fashioned after Alderan's keep," Xith explained. "Only the old sections of the palace though. The maze of passageways used by the King's family should all be unguarded. Surely you've walked them a thousand times..." Xith's voice trailed off.

Adrina smiled, she could walk those passageways in her sleep. Then she frowned.

"But—" she began.

Xith cut her off saying, "Once safely inside and set upon the path, you and Vilmos will remain behind. Emel and I will proceed from there. Do not worry, if the prince lives, we *will* find him. Getting out of the city will be the problem..."

***

As anticipated, the southern sectors of the city were nearly deserted. The four, now on foot, blended into the shadows of cobbled streets as best they could. Emel clearly had not wanted to leave Ebony behind, but eventually he had. Twice they had made their way past patrols without mishap. Fortunately both patrols had been racing north where the battle for the city raged.

Intermittently, Adrina's eyes flashed on the small form of the boy, Vilmos, who walked beside her. He seemed a likeable lad, but a bit young and surely inexperienced. She could see open terror mirrored in his eyes, and more than once he had reached out his hand to hers to find comfort. But Adrina too found comfort in his touch and in the rapier still in its sheath that she clutched with her right hand.

Emel had the lead, and at about ten paces ahead, Adrina could only glimpse his form as he passed the infrequent lights of the darkened city. Somewhere behind them Adrina knew Xith lurked. Many times Xith had disappeared down a side street to reappear beside them at the next intersection.

Adrina gulped for air and her heart skipped as Emel suddenly appeared out of the darkness.

"Patrol," he hissed, "they head south, not north."

Emel flashed his eyes at Xith. Xith waved them into a nearby alleyway.

Huddled in the shadows of the alleyway they waited. Soon, Adrina heard heavy footfalls, then she saw torchlight and shadowed faces. The patrol stopped at the intersection of the street and the alley, directly in front of the horrified onlookers. Adrina heard harsh whispers and angry voices. The members of the patrol were obviously displeased about being sent to watch the city's southern gate while the battle raged elsewhere.

From her vantage point in the shadows, Adrina could see much more than the outlines of faces. Light from their torches reflected dully off their armor and the swords withdrawn from their sheaths. The angry man who seemed the leader of the patrol was bearded and though rather gaunt, just from the tone of his voice and the way he stood, Adrina was sure he was capable with a blade and hardhearted. He was arguing with another man who wanted to return to the north. Both men's words were becoming increasingly belligerent.

Then, to Adrina's horror, the leader of the patrol set upon the other man. In one swift move, he brought the point of his blade to the other's throat and plunged it inward. Adrina screamed, which would have brought sure discovery, if Emel hadn't clasped a hand to her mouth just prior. As it was, her muffled scream mixed with the horrible gurgling sounds of the dying man as he sought to speak a few last words.

The leader removed his sword from the other's throat as he fell, and without another word, the members of his patrol continued south.

Emel removed his hand from Adrina's mouth and put his hands on her shoulders. "Are you all right, Adrina?" he whispered.

Adrina couldn't answer. She felt numb and sick.

"It will pass, Adrina," Emel said. "As I said, 'This is not the practice field.' This is real. Are you all right with that?"

Adrina still couldn't answer. Emel shook her.

"Adrina will be all right in a moment," Xith said. "Give her some breathing room."

Xith took Adrina's hand.

"We near the city center," whispered Xith. "Once past the last line of buildings there will be no cover. On my signal move quickly and without stopping across the square to the walls of the keep. Emel, you'll go first. Then, Vilmos. Then, Adrina. Once at the wall, speak not a word. Await my signal to continue..."

***

At a flat-out run, Adrina raced across the square. Her heart was pounding in her ears. Vilmos and Emel had already made it safely across the open hundred yards to the shadowed wall and were excitedly watching her run. Adrina glanced from Emel to the archers on the walls. Only one of them needed to spot her and it would all be for nothing.

Halfway across, Adrina no longer held back her smile. The run was strangely exhilarating after the tension of creeping through the besieged city. She glanced back once to look for Xith. She knew he waited somewhere out of sight behind her to make the last mad dash across the square. When Adrina glanced back, her foot caught one of the square's cobblestones. She tumbled and fell. Her face struck cold stones.

Disoriented, she looked up. Emel was edging away from the safety of the wall. She waved him away. Then her eyes rose to the top of the wall, a single figure stood looking down over the square now, seemingly his eyes looked straight at her. Breathless, Adrina waited for him to raise an alarm or notch an arrow to the string of his bow.

Unmoving, Adrina waited, and waited. The archer stood still. He stared down into the darkness of the square. For an instant, it seemed their eyes locked. The archer raised one of his arms— surely he was about to reach into the quiver at his side for an arrow. Adrina's heart stopped and the whole of the world seemingly collapsed in around her. Adrina stifled a moan, held her breath and waited.

As the archer turned away and continued his march along the battlements of the wall, Adrina thanked Great-Father for smiling down upon her and launched herself into a run.

Hastened by her fright, she crossed the remaining distance to the wall in a surprising burst of speed. Emel caught her in his arms and held her for a moment before both turned to look back across the square. Immediate shock registered on their faces, Xith stood in plain sight in the middle of the square.

Adrina heard Vilmos whisper, "Run, run." Then he began waving his arms wildly to the shaman. Heedless, Xith waved them on. "*Go now,*" he said in a voice that was strangely compelling and seemed to carry across the square on the wind, *Do what you must...*

❧ The Kingdoms & The Elves ❧

A cry went up from the walls and suddenly a number of voices were echoing an alarm. Almost immediately afterward Adrina heard the twang of bows and the hiss of arrows. She squeezed her eyes tight. Fool, she thought to herself, sacrificing himself for no gain.

"Quickly now," said the boy, Vilmos, seeming suddenly resolved to action. "Pray my master's diversion buys our way into the inner keep…" His words fell away, and, as if in response to his voice, a blue-white streak raced through the air to the wall. Disquieting screams followed.

One of the archers fell from atop the wall and smacked the cobblestones not more than five feet from where Adrina stood. The man's face was twisted oddly toward her. The emptiness in his eyes and the unnatural twist of his body told Adrina the fall had been fatal.

More blue-white streaks raced to the wall. Another soldier fell to his death—Adrina saw no trace of the blue-flighted arrows that had claimed either man. Emel grabbed Adrina's hand and pulled her after him.

The minutes that followed were crazed and everything for a time afterward passed in a blur. Adrina found herself racing alongside Emel and Vilmos. She remembered remarking that the buildings of the inner keep truly did resemble the old wings of Imtal Palace and that true to Xith's word, the King's entryway into the main building was unguarded. She lead them along unlit passageways that were familiar to her feet even in darkness, yet she knew they only seemed that way.

It wasn't until many uncertain minutes later that Adrina

abruptly halted. She realized she no longer heard voices and that the footsteps she was running away from were her own and that of her companions. When she stopped, first Vilmos and then Emel slammed into her.

"What's wrong?" asked Emel.

"Nothing," Adrina said in a hiss. She turned to Vilmos. "Did Xith tell either of you where they would hold my brother?"

Even in muted darkness, Adrina could see the boy shrug.

"I thought he told you," Emel said.

After a long silence, Vilmos spoke. "Xith said it would be easy and that getting out of the city would be the hard part. Your instinct is what led you here in the first place. Where were you going?"

Another period of silence followed, then Adrina said, "I really have roamed these passageways a thousand times. They are a solitary place. My father never liked them and doesn't use them. It is true that very few even know they exist."

"Where were you going?" repeated Vilmos.

Adrina continued as if she hadn't heard the question. "I wonder if... No, that would be too much to hope for." Vilmos glared at her. "I guess, I was going to my quarters."

Vilmos suggested that she should continue.

Adrina closed her eyes in thought for a moment, then lead them on their way. After ascending a flight of stairs and after a few twists and turns in the passageway, the three found themselves standing before a door. Only Adrina knew for certain what was beyond the door, the others could only guess. She slid the door open, expecting to find her room.

She was about to step into the room, when Emel swept past her, a short blade cupped in his right hand. There was a rather large man standing hunched over with his back to the door only a few feet away. Emel stealthily crept up on him and plied the blade to his throat. Then he spun the man around.

Adrina bit her tongue to stop her scream. Then as she sought to speak no words came forth. Her eyes were wild and Emel stared at her for a moment in apparent confusion.

"Adrina?"

"Valam," Adrina said. "By the Mother, you live." Adrina was crying now and she ran to embrace her brother.

Shocked, Emel lowered the blade from the prince's throat. "Dear Father—Your Highness, forgive me. I had no idea."

Valam embraced Adrina in a great bear hug and swept her from her feet. His joy was short-lived, his expression grew suddenly grim and he let Adrina go. "It is not safe here, you must go."

"But, we are here to rescue you."

The prince put a finger to his sister's lips. "There are things occurring here that you cannot hope to understand. You must leave at once."

"What is wrong with you, Valam? Come quickly." No sooner had Adrina said this than someone off to the side of the room cleared their throat. Adrina turned and from an adjacent doorway, great blue eyes greeted her. Adrina asked, "Prince William?"

The other nodded and grinned evilly.

"Run, Adrina, run," Valam said. He flung Adrina toward the passageway and barreled at the prince.

Complete pandemonium followed. Confused, Emel and Vilmos stood their ground. Adrina recovered her feet and stared in wonder at the struggle between her brother and Prince William. Valam had a firm grip on the other's throat. William was straining to reach a short blade in his belt.

Adrina watched in mute horror as Prince William broke free of her brother's grasp and whirled about to face him. Prince Valam was nearly the largest man in the Kingdom. With bare fists he could take any man, but where Prince Valam had only his fists, the other had a long, curved blade made for close-quarters fighting.

Two guards rushed into the room. Again Adrina tried to scream and no words came out. Seeing the guards, Emel sprang forward and engaged both.

Undaunted by the menacing blade, Valam circled defensively, waiting to attack. William it seemed was also waiting for the right moment to strike. The end came quick and clean, Prince William sliced in with his blade, Valam countered and then planted a solid blow to the side of the other's unprotected skull. Prince William went down, his knees crumbling, his body collapsing beneath him.

More guards swept upon them from the open doorway. Emel screamed wildly and pointed to the passageway. Vilmos remained deathly still, apparently gripped by fear. Adrina turned. Soldiers were streaming out of the tunnel behind her. Before she could get free, one had her arm and twisted it back forcefully, a burning pain shot up to her elbow.

Prince Valam descended upon the attackers like a hungry demon, his eyes unfocused and angry. He grabbed the man that held Adrina by the throat, lifted him off the floor and flung him to the wall. Without stopping, Valam slapped Emel's blade away and backed Adrina, Vilmos and Emel into the corner. He stood guardedly in front of them.

With the aid of two guards, Prince William regained his feet. He rubbed the side of his head and directed a vengeful stare at Valam.

Valam maintained the face-off against the many guards in the room and directed his eyes at William. "Tell them to back off," Valam shouted, "we'll submit!"

"Enough, enough," William said. He clapped his hands together and the soldiers backed away. "Stay your ground. Let's shed no more blood than we need to for now.... We have what we wanted, and a prize or two to boot."

Chapter Eight:
Prisoners

Through the night Father Jacob watched the strange one, the one called Seth. As the shaman had asked, Jacob placed the healing stones one by one to Seth's forehead. He had seen such stones before in the Temple of the Mother, but never had he witnessed their ability to heal. When first held the strange stones hummed and glowed bright yellow, touched to Seth's forehead, the color slowly drained from them until they were left dull, black and empty.

Suddenly, two hours before dawn, Seth had opened his eyes and spoken. "Where is my companion?" he had asked, his words in the old language.

The old language, being the language of priests and priestesses, hadn't surprised Jacob. He had answered without thought in the same tongue. "I do not know, I am sorry."

It was only now that Father Jacob was deep in conversation with Seth that he realized Seth spoke in the old tongue, the language that had once been universal to all peoples and was now preserved only by those of the Mother and Father. Jacob considered Seth's statement for a moment more, then replied. "Then it is true, you are an elf."

There is disbelief in your voice, Fa-a-ther—Seth stumbled over the word—he had told Jacob earlier that he didn't feel comfortable naming a Man father. —*Jacob, yet your thoughts say you want to understand.*

"Myth and lore would have most Kingdomers believe that your kind are akin to fairies, pixies and sprites."

Seth smiled and regarded Jacob with his blue eyes. He seemed to know Jacob was joking.

Jacob continued. "You must meet a friend of mine. Keeper Martin would write entire tomes filled with your words. There would be a definite gleam in his eyes as he wrote: elf of the gold and green forest, most fair and generous…"

Yes Jacob, I am very much mortal, just as you, Seth said, answering the question that had been on Jacob's mind for some time. *Many of my companions journeyed to Great-Father so that I could be here, and it fills my heart with sorrow to know it was all for nothing…*

"You will have counsel before King Andrew, friend Seth, this I promise you."

"*You do not understand, without my companion, Brother Galan, I have failed. My fate is here… She was needed to return to my homeland, the land of East Reach.*

"There is something you must know, Brother Seth," Jacob said, borrowing the title as it seemed appropriate. "The one who found you said something that was strange. On the beach where you were found, it appeared there had been a struggle of some sort. One dead man attested to this. Unless there was a man in your party?"

There were no Men— Seth's voice sounded suddenly distant. His eyes flashed, his expression became one of puzzled remembrance. *Yes, yes there it is.* Seth sent surprise and hope into Jacob's mind along with the words.

For the first time Father Jacob realized Seth spoke in thoughts and not aloud. Do you walk in my thoughts? He asked himself.

It is the way of my people. I took open thought as a sign that you wanted me to enter your mind. I am sorry if I have offended you.

"Nothing of the sort, Brother Seth," Jacob said, "you continue to surprise me is all. There really are poor records of the four peoples after the Race Wars."

Tell me of this other, the one who found me and the one you are thinking of now. He is of the four peoples, is he not?

"Xith, last of the Watchers. I first met him thirteen years ago. He came to me in a time of great need. He promised he would return one day when the need was again great, and he has. Great Kingdom is being consumed by the heart of darkness itself."

Would he know where Galan is?

Jacob nodded in understanding. "He might, he just might, but I suspect the disappearance of your friend is tied to the struggle we face. Xith said that we were drawn to you because of a joining of the paths. Our fates are together, my friend."

And more I am afraid. I remember some of it now. At the last, I called out with my mind in desperation. The call, I fear, lead more than just those who wished to aid me. I fear I summoned your enemy as well, and now they've taken Galan.

Seth attempted to stand and did so only with Jacob's help. *I would help you. What must I do?*

"For now, there is little we can do. If Xith has not returned to camp shortly after sunrise, we journey north and return with the King's army marshaled before us."

Jacob looked to the East where dawn was forming on the horizon. "To war," he whispered. "But for now we can only wait and hope against hope... I truly fear the worst."

***

For two days Captain Trendmore drove the column north along the coast of the great sea. On smooth terrain the foot soldiers maintained a steady pace and made good progress. Keeper Martin was hopeful that by afternoon the walls and spires of the Free Cities would be in sight.

Doubt had grown in the Lore Keeper from the moment the column had turned north instead of south, but Martin had no definite proof to act on his feelings. He couldn't act on hunches and doubts. For all he knew Captain Trendmore was indeed following Captain Brodst's orders. But then again, if he didn't take action, who would?

Keeper Martin cast a sidelong glance at the close-mouthed rider to his left, then lowered the hood of his cloak and looked to the sea. A strong breeze out of the north carried with it a salty spray. "On such a hot day," Martin said, "the moisture and the breeze are refreshing. Don't you think so, captain?"

Captain Adylton replied, "The sun near midday is hot here, Lore Keeper, you would do well to keep that hood about your head."

Martin eyed the tall, dark-skinned Southerner who had removed his cloak about an hour into the ride and rode with short leggings that exposed calves and knees.

Captain Adylton quickly added, "Playing in the surf and lying by the sea is about all I did in my youth. My father was a fisher..."

Keeper Martin smiled—a mischievous smile. In a voice that barely carried above the plodding of his mount's hooves, he asked, "Did you sail these waters often with your father then?"

"More often than I cared to."

Martin noted Captain Adylton's annoyance and his apparent wish to end the conversation. "Would an autumn storm have driven your sails north or south?"

"I see," Adylton said, "that troubles you too."

Martin nodded. "I have sailed to High Province close to winter season many times. Always I felt the breezes upon my face when I stood at the bow."

"Aye, the winds change with the ending of summer. Autumn and winter bring cold breezes out the north."

"Captain Trendmore wasn't a fisher's son was he?" Martin asked.

"Hardly, his father was a tanner or was it a smithy—at any rate, no, I'm sure he's never sailed."

"I have known Captain Brodst for many years, yet I cannot recall his father's trade?"

Captain Adylton gave Keeper Martin a stern look. "You know as well as I that..." The captain's voice trailed off. He looked again at Martin, suddenly seeming to realize where Martin was going with his questions. "You are right. The storms would have blown the ship south if it strayed off course at all. Any experienced captain would have had little trouble in those storms. They were early autumn storms, full of malice yes, but not violent like the storms of winter."

Keeper Martin looked Captain Adylton straight in the eye. "Do you have loyal men in your squadron?"

Captain Adylton stared back at Martin. "They are loyal men all, and they follow all lawful orders of their commanding officers. None would turn against the other, if that is your hope."

"What of unlawful orders given by a man who is no longer loyal to his country or his countrymen?"

Captain Adylton reined in his steed, nearly coming to a halt. "Proving such a thing, Keeper—" His changing the pace brought mayhem to those in the column behind him. A wagon driver's team nearly drove over him. Captain Adylton shrugged off the man's curses and spurred his mount. "—How do you propose to do that?"

Keeper Martin judged the captain's receptiveness to the truth by the unease in his eyes. "There is news I have not shared with you, captain. The situation is much graver than you are aware of. It was not just the upcoming departure of a ship from the port city of Wellison that brought me to Imtal Palace to disturb King Andrew's rest in the middle of the night. Prior to this, I had been in the Far South for many months. Secretly.

"At first it was personal matters that brought me to Sever more than anything else. After, much more. It was fortunate that only Keeper Q'yer of Quashan' knew my whereabouts. Also fortunate that my last visit to Sever had been some years before.

"When I arrived in Gregortonn, all seemed well. The affairs in the capital were running smoothly. Overnight, all this changed. King Charles ordered the city sealed. The city garrison turned to the streets. Hundreds were arrested. Dozens killed in clashes. For a full day afterward the city was quiet. Only the flags removed from their poles upon the walls attested to turmoil. Then just before dawn of the second day, the searches began. More arrests, more fighting. Luckily I was able to find reliable accommodations, which did not come without a price.

"Two weeks I was in hiding, plotting my escape. Then one afternoon while moving to a new safe house, I made a most unexpected discovery. Soldiers loyal to King Charles were no longer in control of the city. An agent of King Jarom had usurped power… Everything I'd seen suddenly made sense.

"Soon after I arrived in the new safe house one of my benefactors discovered my true identity. I don't know how, but it was a fortunate turn of events, for it was then that men loyal to Charles approached me. They spoke of a bold plan to retake the city and of a plan to smuggle the heir to the throne from the city to safety. It was with their help that I eventually made my way back to Great Kingdom."

Keeper Martin took a long swig from a wineskin, then cleared his throat. "You know as well as I that King Charles' voice was the only vote of dissension in the Minors when King Jarom last sued for war and the dissolution of the Kingdom Alliance. His aim is war with Great Kingdom, there can be no doubt."

Again Captain Adylton disrupted the pace of the group, he reined in his mount and stared at Keeper Martin. The wagon driver behind the captain screamed angrily this time.

"Is there something wrong?" came an excited voice from behind them. A rider raced toward them. Both Martin and Adylton recognized the voice and the rider, Captain Trendmore.

"We must act, are we agreed on that, Captain Adylton?" Martin asked as he raised the hood of his cloak.

Captain Adylton signaled agreement and urged his mount onward.

"Is there something wrong here?" Captain Trendmore repeated when he came abreast of the two.

"I was just explaining to the good keeper that if he kept his face to the sun for another hour on a day like today, he would be as bright as a one of Duke Ispeth's apples before nightfall. I think it took him by surprise."

"Yes, yes indeed," Captain Trendmore said, a crooked smile coming to his lips.

***

It was the morning of the second day since their capture and still Vilmos cursed himself. Xith had told him to do what he must and he had done nothing. To him this was unacceptable and as he marched with his hands tied painfully tight behind his back, he hung his head in shame. It seemed of small consequence to know that Prince William and his henchmen had fled Alderan out of fear they might not be able to control the city any longer.

Vilmos knew little of the Prince of the North, Valam, but he was sure there had been tears in his eyes when William of Sever had ordered the city set ablaze and that no building should be left standing. That night, even from miles and miles away, they had seen the unearthly glow of the burning city. Vilmos had seen rage and hatred in Prince Valam's eyes then.

They had been moving since daybreak without respite. The first day they had stayed near the coast, traveling south, but this day they traveled more east than south. Vilmos knew this because the sun shined almost directly in his eyes, making the world around him bleached and hazy. He knew only that Princess Adrina was to his right and that if he didn't maintain a correct pace, he stepped on the heels of the guardsman, Emel.

Sweat dripping down from his forehead ran irritatingly into his eyes, and, with his hands tied behind his back, Vilmos couldn't wipe it away. Exhaustion sought to overcome him and he fought to stay alert. He still held hope that Xith would somehow rescue them.

An abrupt kick from behind sent Vilmos sprawling. Screaming, he hit the hard ground face first. He spun around angrily and spat out dirt.

"Rest," said the voice of the figure towering above him.

With his back now to the sun, Vilmos found the haze in front of his eyes slowly clearing. He stared up at the shadowed figure, which hovered over him for a moment more before turning away.

"Are you all right?" Adrina asked.

Vilmos said, "I think so." His backside was a little sore but he'd recover. His pride was hurt more than anything. He had done nothing to provoke William's men yet it seemed they had singled him out. More than anyone else, Vilmos bore the brunt of their resentment and anger. He was the one who was forced to watch while the others ate, albeit meagerly. He was the one who was denied water or forced to drink from a bowl like an animal. He was the one who was pushed and kicked.

The brooding prince also regarded him. "You are tougher than you look, my young friend, I am glad." Prince Valam was silent for a moment, then continued. "It seems you have been singled out because you are the smallest and the youngest. Their aim is to break you and thus break us all. Know that I *will* give repayment for every such mistreatment. And know also, that many a man would have already yielded."

Emel seemed to agree. He winked at Vilmos. "Hang in there, we will surely make them pay."

"May Queen Elthia turn over in her grave so that she does not have to see the harvest her son seeks," Vilmos whispered. Prince Valam turned a puzzled frown to Vilmos. "My father's words," Vilmos explained.

"It seems we were never properly introduced, my young friend. You look of royal blood and you speak like one well educated and Kingdom borne. Yet, I have never seen you in any of the southern courts beside your father."

Vilmos' faced flushed red. "I am hardly of royal blood, my father is a village counselor." Vilmos paused, his tongue growing flustered. "In truth, I am ill at ease in your company..." His voice trailed off momentarily.

"Yours too, Princess," Vilmos said, turning to Adrina briefly before turning back to Prince Valam. "And in truth, I am not as tough as you might think. I was more afraid of crying in your presence than of my lost pride. Even William of Sever's men respect you."

"Respect and fear are two different things, Vilmos. They fear me only as long as we remain on Kingdom soil. Matters will change when we reach Sever." Prince Valam turned at the sound of approaching footsteps. "Water," he shouted at the guard. "Water for everyone!"

***

The passing of another day brought Vilmos only more misery. Prince Valam had told him that perhaps tomorrow they would enter the northernmost forests of the Kingdom of Sever. Vilmos had cringed at the mention of the Vangar, yet it seemed he had always known he would one day return there. Now, even as he closed his eyes and tried to find sleep, he saw the great white fangs and glowing eyes of the beasts called Wolmerrelle.

As the night looked to be a cold one, Vilmos, Adrina, Valam and Emel huddled close for warmth. They bedded down upon the hard ground and could only look with yearning at the fires a short distance away. They had been offered neither blankets nor fire, which was in stark contrast to the previous days.

Behind him, Vilmos could hear whispers passing back and forth between Emel and Adrina. Afraid to close his eyes, Vilmos stared into the darkness and listened in. He wasn't surprised to find they were talking about William of Sever once again.

"I don't understand," Adrina was saying, "the lady told us to find him. As if all would be well once we did. She said he would not arrive in Alderan…"

Emel corrected the princess, "She said the ship would not arrive in Alderan and that only death awaited there. We did not listen and look what has happened. Have you told anyone else of that conversation?

"Only Father Jacob… And, Xith…"

Emel was silent for a time, and Vilmos almost fell asleep against his will. "Should we tell His Highness, perhaps together… No, it is a foolish hope."

"Go on," said another voice. Prince Valam edged closer, pressing Vilmos, who was between the giant and Emel, closer to Emel. "I have long wondered why Prince William would turn against us. Our kingdoms have always been the strongest of allies…"

Vilmos wanted to say something but held back.

"Perhaps we should post a watch. This is something no one else was meant to hear," whispered Adrina.

"Emel," Valam whispered, and the guardsman inched away into the night, leaving only the three.

As Adrina began her tale of the meetings with the lady of the night, Vilmos' thoughts started to wander. He had heard this story once already.

The next thing Vilmos knew Emel was returning. He didn't know how much time had elapsed or what had transpired in the interim, though he suspected somewhere along the line he had fallen asleep.

"They sleep," Emel said. "Now there are only guards around the periphery."

Valam continued to speak without pausing, "Perhaps it wasn't Prince William you dreamed of. What of these others? This Xith you spoke of, perhaps it was him."

"Perhaps," Adrina said. She didn't sound convinced.

"Perhaps not," Vilmos whispered to himself just before sleep found him.

***

With morning came rain, a ceaseless downpouring that made the day all the drearier. To make matters worse, the soft breeze out of the North that had been with them for days was by midday a steady gale. It brought with it a hint of winter's chill. To Vilmos it didn't matter that winter was still months away, he was chilled to the bone all the same. He longed for his hooded cloak, a place next to a warm and cheerful fire, and a bowl of winter stew.

The only good thing about this day was that his hands were free, and although Prince Valam said it was yet another sign that William and his men were becoming increasingly bold and less and less afraid, Vilmos didn't care. He only knew how good it felt to have the restraints off his wrists.

Apparently seeing Vilmos' peaked appearance, Prince Valam handed Vilmos his overtunic. Vilmos was hesitant to take it.

Vilmos said, "You'll catch your death of cold, Your Highness."

"Snows in High Province are already knee-deep, and in winter they are so deep a man cannot walk across them. Take it, Vilmos, to me it will make little difference. The hide is specially treated, rain will not soak it. It will keep you from catching a cold. When the time for action comes we'll need everyone at their best."

Vilmos accepted the tunic and wrapped it about him. The Prince's overtunic was so big in fact that Vilmos was able to wear it like he would have his hooded cloak. He didn't put his hands into the sleeves. Instead, he pulled the collar up over his head and peered out through a space between the two middle ties.

Vilmos trudged on. Hours passed. Afternoon came. Still, rain poured down upon them. Then just when Vilmos thought the day would end much as it had begun, his deepest fears were realized. The green of forest came into sight.

It was then, in a softly whispered voice that Vilmos told the prince, the princess and the guardsman of his previous travels in the Vangar. He also told them of the soldiers in the valley, and of the Wolmerrelle. All the while he spoke, an uncontrollable trembling and dread flooded over him.

"Thank you, Vilmos," Prince Valam said. For a time he was obviously deep in thought, then Valam said, "Be that as it may, we must address other matters. Once we cross the boundaries of the Kingdom into the Minors, our captor will have little use for you and Emel.

"I know not why he has allowed Emel to live, but I am sure now why you live. He is using you to keep me in check. He knew I would brood over the injustices he has given you and think not of other things—escape. That is exactly what I did. His advisors whisper well in his ear.

"But my mind is clouded no more. Tomorrow in the forest," Valam said, "we *will* make our move then. To die fighting is honorable. To die with a blade in your back is quite another thing..."

Emel seemed to agree. "Tomorrow," he whispered.

Vilmos wanted to say that Vangar Forest was no place for travelers, especially a small group of unarmed travelers on the run. Instead, he found himself saying, "William of Sever is at home in the forest more than any man. It wouldn't be a wise—"

Emel cut in. "Would you rather die then?"

Adrina, who had been regarding Vilmos thoughtfully, spoke before he could respond to Emel, "You call the Prince 'William of Sever' and there is a ring in your voice as if you know him."

As if suddenly realizing a thing that had passed by him, Prince Valam's eyebrows rose and he nodded his head contemplatively. "You are right." He turned to Vilmos. "Have you met William before?"

"My father is the Counselor of Tabborrath Village."

"You are Minor-born," Adrina said. "And you have met him before?"

"Not directly, though I once saw him at the Three Village Assembly. Everyone from our village circle and many from the forests came to Olex Village that day. It was the first time William of Sever had returned to his birthplace."

"Birthplace?" Valam said, disbelief in his voice. "Queen Elthia was my mother's sister. She was not Minor-born."

Vilmos started to say something but Emel cut him off with a wave of his hand. Almost immediately afterward, Vilmos went sprawling face first into the muddy ground as he was booted from behind.

"Rest," said the now familiar voice. The guard, who apparently took great pleasure in his misdeed, turned away laughing as Vilmos spat and tried to wipe mud from his eyes.

This time as Valam screamed at the guards, "Bring water," none of them moved.

"Already they find bravery," Prince Valam whispered, "perhaps tonight in the forest would be even better."

"You give the word, Your Highness, and only death will keep me from your side," Emel said.

"I do not think they will kill the two of you just yet. If you truly are Minor-born, Vilmos," Valam said, turning as he spoke, "William may just give you your life. Use that chance, Vilmos, use it for all it's worth. Go back to Tabborrath Village and leave the affairs of men to men."

Vilmos felt suddenly stung. He turned away, hiding the tears in his eyes.

Adrina sat beside Vilmos. She spoke softly to him. "You were about to answer my brother's question. What were you going to say?"

"Nothing," Vilmos said through his tears.

Apparently Prince Valam noted Vilmos' tears too, for as he spoke his voice, which had never been truly gentle before, was also soft. "Go on, please…"

Vilmos shifted to a more comfortable sitting position. "William of Sever was not born in Gregortonn. Gregortonn is the capital, it is not a place of birth."

Seemingly remembering something from the past, Adrina laughed, "Chancellor Yi's lessons…" Her voice trailed off and for a moment it seemed she wasn't going to explain. "All births are registered according to the ancestral home of the father. For census, tithe and tax."

"Of course," Vilmos said. He found he was smiling. "My father muttered many silent curses in its name. It was the only of his responsibilities that he disliked."

Emel waved a hand under his chin. The conversation stopped.

Vilmos turned and saw a guard approaching.

"To your feet!" shouted a gruff voice, signifying an end to the brief rest. Apparently their captors were eager for the feeling of safety being within the borders of Sever would provide.

Vilmos struggled to his feet, and stared glumly at Prince Valam momentarily. Then his thoughts turned quickly to what lay ahead. Whatever their struggle, it would take place in the Vangar. Vilmos was sure of this now as he had been sure of no other thing.

Chapter Nine:
Bushwhacked

Like thieves in the night the enemy army had stolen upon Quashan'. From atop the city's fortified walls, Chancellor Van'te stared out at the enemy host. In the two days since their arrival, they had staged no attacks against the city and though they barred all travel into or out of the city, they harassed its residents in no other way.

Chancellor Van'te turned to the young sergeant at arms beside him. "How many do you estimate today?"

Sergeant Danyel' grimaced. "A few hundred more arrived in the night. Still, nearly the same as yesterday, around ten thousand."

"That is my estimate also." Van'te looked glumly to the young recruits on the wall. "How many were you able to rouse to the city defenses?"

"Two hundred more," Danyel' said proudly. "I told them nothing of the garrison's absence. None would have believed me anyway, who would believe the entire garrison, save for the handful which includes me, is gone."

The chancellor scrutinized the sergeant, then said in a soft voice, "You think me the true fool to allow such an order to pass, don't you?"

"The seal was genuine, and what man can refuse a summons by his King. Perhaps Imtal is likewise besieged."

Chancellor Van'te wasn't able to respond. "Runner!" came the cry from the west wall.

Chancellor Van'te grinned, he knew if he were persistent enough one of his messengers would get through. "Give the man some help!" Van'te shouted to the archers on the walls. As archers began firing wildly at the enemy line out of their range, the chancellor moved to leave the wall. "Sergeant Danyel'," he said, "lead me from the wall."

The two hurriedly made their way to the courtyard where they hoped to find good news. It was a short walk. Still Chancellor Van'te, well advanced in his years, found he was wheezing and puffing by the walk's end.

When Van'te and Danyel' reached the courtyard, they found the runner winded and hunched over after his sprint across the field. Still, without delay the runner handed Chancellor Van'te the scroll, and in earnest the chancellor began to read its contents. "By the Father, " Van'te muttered to himself, "it is from Prince Valam..." His voice trailed off and shock registered on his face.

Chancellor Yi turned to say something to the runner and found the man gone, as if he had vanished. "Sergeant Danyel'," Van'te screamed in a high-pitched nasal tone as only he could, "I want that runner found!"

Danyel' signaled to the two soldiers beside him. They hurried off. Danyel' asked, "What does it say? Is the message truly from His Highness?"

Chancellor Van'te showed the scroll to Danyel'. A mute minute passed, then the sergeant said, "Are you sure this is truly Prince Valam's writing? Couldn't this be an elaborate hoax to make us quit the city?"

A pained expression crossed Van'te's face. He blamed himself for what had transpired. He felt suddenly tired and old. "I have schooled His Highness all the years of his life. Surely by now, I should be able to recognize his scrawl... See the loops above the I's, the double slashes on the T's and the way he stops to make an L?"

Danyel' nodded.

"Done that since he was a boy first learning to write, just to annoy me—Yes, I am sure it is his handwriting."

"Do you really believe that if we opened the gates of the city, the army surrounding Quashan' would guarantee safe passage for all who wished to leave?"

"Prince Valam didn't."

Danyel' seemed confused. "What do you mean?"

Chancellor Van'te flattened out the scroll and pointed to the last few lines.

Danyel said, "I still don't understand."

"The handwriting switched here... Can you see the darkening of the strokes?" Danyel' shook his head. "Never mind, never mind. Only a foolish old man or a young boy such as you would think five hundred could defend a city from ten thousand."

"You, Chancellor Van'te, are no fool," Danyel' said. He patted the chancellor on the back. "If any can save Quashan', it is you. Tell us what you would have us do, and we will do it."

"At any rate, there is little we can do now. Soon enough they'll know we do not intend to quit the city, the attack will begin then..."

***

Prince Valam turned to Emel. "How many men are stationed around the periphery of the camp?"

"You mean, is there hope for escape this night?" Emel leaned close to Valam and whispered something that Adrina couldn't hear, but, from the expression on her brother's face, it wasn't good news. Adrina returned to her muddled thoughts. Since their capture, her thoughts had been ever jumbled and never clear.

A day of trudging along overgrown paths had left her exhausted and in tears. Mostly she was distraught because she had always considered herself capable of doing anything a man could do, yet every day now she saw how much she depended on Emel and Valam to make it through the day—especially this last day. Here she had found a bitter truth, until now her life had been the pampered and sheltered life of a spoiled little girl.

Adrina was also agitated because it seemed Valam and Emel left her out of their plans for escape. Disappointed, she remembered a conversation she had with Emel days ago, just before Alderan. She had told him, "I am as good with a blade as you are, perhaps better..."

Emel had replied, "Besting me on the practice field is not the same thing, Adrina." She remembered how coldly Emel had said it, and how bitter the truth of it was now that she understood what he had meant.

Again she heard the words of the mysterious lady in her ears. *The evil brings the change you so wished for. It has found a home in the emptiness of your heart. You care too little for those around you. You see not the servants who toil for you, workers in the fields on their hands and knees with the whip at their backs, drudges scouring the kitchen floors... You must open your eyes!*

Adrina thought back to another time, and when she closed her eyes she saw the quiet fields of Mellack Proper—it was then only two days after she met the mysterious lady and her journey was only beginning. Lying there on the cold ground, her body sore, her stomach rumbling, the fields of Mellack Proper, the orchards of Duke Ispeth, the hills of the Braddabaggon and even the mires of Lord Fraddylwicke all seemed desperately far away.

Adrina rubbed painfully blistered feet. "My eyes are open, *truly* open," she whispered to the wind. Opening her eyes meant much more than simply seeing the things around her. It meant looking for and finding understanding in the world around her, looking not only with her eyes but also with her heart, mind and soul, and then finding resolve to action. It meant being a participant instead of an onlooker.

"Adrina!" hissed Emel in her ear, breaking Adrina from her thoughts.

Adrina started, Emel clasped a hand over her mouth. Adrina noticed then that the camp seemed suddenly shrouded in darkness. Beneath the forest canopy no stars were visible. Even the central fire seemed muted by the stark darkness. Then she noted that the logs on the fire were all but fiery ashes. Apparently many hours had passed in what to her had seemed minutes. "Yes?" Adrina finally answered.

Emel squeezed her hand. Just then Adrina noticed the ropes that had been tied around her feet and hands were gone. Before she could speak her thoughts Emel nodded his head as if he were reading them. Her eyes went wide. Adrina tried to speak again. Emel put a silencing finger to her lips.

Valam gripped her shoulder and turned Adrina to face him. He showed her four fingers and then pointing to Emel, he lowered three. With two fingers raised, he pointed to her. Three to Vilmos whose eyes were as wide as saucers. Four, Valam pointed to himself.

He then turned her head to look around the camp. In the distance Adrina saw the immense trunks of the great southern trees whose intertwined boughs formed the clearing they were in. At the far edge of the camp a number of watch fires were set, but they also burned low. Only a handful of guards still stood their watch. Valam pointed out two of them. In the dim light Adrina watched them. One kept slapping both hands to his face, apparently trying to erase sleep from his tired eyes. The other was leaning up against a tree and, to some degree, faced their direction.

A long period of complete silence passed as they waited, for what Adrina wasn't entirely sure. Then, without preface, Valam raised a single finger and Emel slipped away. For an instant afterward, Adrina saw Emel's silhouette against light cast by the fading fires and then he disappeared into the unshadowed gloom.

Adrina held her breath as Valam gripped her shoulder.

Unexpectedly he embraced her, and for a moment Adrina was smothered in his great embrace, then, just as suddenly, he ushered her into the gloom after Emel. Her thoughts swam, Adrina didn't move. Valam gave her a push and suddenly she was racing along the ground on her hands and knees.

Many times she cast nervous sidelong glances to the center of the camp and to the nearest two guards at the perimeter. Any minute she expected someone to shout an alarm and the camp to burst into frenzied activity. As fear and anxiety sought to overwhelm her, Adrina fought to hold them in check.

She knew she had finally reached the edge of the camp when the trunk of one of the great trees appeared in front of her. The next thing Adrina knew, friendly hands were gripping her waist and pulling her to her feet. She didn't pull away from Emel's embrace. Instead she hugged him fiercely. His warmth was the only reassuring thing she had known for days and now it was even more reassuring.

Silently Emel and Adrina waited. The next face Adrina hoped to see was that of the boy, Vilmos. Slowly over the five days of their captivity, Adrina had come to know Vilmos. To her it seemed a strange darkness lurked behind his eyes and also that his thoughts were ever distant and he was distant. She found this oddly alluring, for in him she saw a bit of herself.

Thinking she saw movement in the gloom, Adrina leaned forward. She knew at once the burly figure she saw wasn't Vilmos. Panic entered her mind and momentarily, the urge to flee. She pushed back against Emel's warmth, her body growing tense.

Abruptly Emel grabbed Adrina and roughly pulled her back

and down. Huddled against the ground they lay together. Adrina saw a figure outlined against the murky pale of the dying lights in the camp. Soon afterward, a second shadowed form joined the first.

"Erravane?" hissed the first. Adrina held deathly still.

The other responded with, "Yes." From the voice alone, Adrina couldn't tell if the second figure was a man or a woman, though the first she thought a man. Among Prince William's soldiers, only a dozen of the several hundred were women. Although they were few, it seemed that they held high positions. Valam had suggested that perhaps they served as William's personal bodyguards, though he had been honestly unsure of this estimation since several of them came and went seemingly at their own leisure.

A long period of silence followed. Adrina couldn't see what transpired, though she knew both figures still stood only a few feet away. Then with a sudden heave, both were on the ground and for a time they rolled around in the leaves. Afterward, again silence. Adrina knew only that Emel's presence beside her was a powerful comfort.

Suddenly Adrina heard muffled laughter and again the whispered voices.

"Quit, you'll alert the camp," hissed the first.

"Not likely."

"What do you mean?" the first sounded at the end of his patience. "Why are you here, Erravane?"

Behind her Adrina heard Emel's barely audible gasp. He had recognized the first voice at nearly the same time as she.

"One question at a time my sweet." Adrina was sure now, the second *was* a woman. Her name was Erravane, and the first *was* Prince William. "I have found what you sought."

"And the traitor?"

"Oh yes, a present for you." Erravane rose to her knees, then dumped something onto the ground. She cackled madly, then said, "His head."

William jumped to his feet. "I trust the other is alive?"

"The southern encampments have proceeded north as planned. The bulk of your army is spread out through the forest. Your commanders will join you here, tomorrow."

"What of King Jarom's army?... Wait a minute, what of the—"

Erravane cut William off, "You are ever impatient. She is well. I believe the deceased—" Erravane kicked the head and it rolled past Adrina. Only Emel's firm and comforting grip around her waist kept Adrina from screaming. "—Was tricked. Though I am not sure how. These creatures have strange powers."

"Then you were right?"

Erravane cooed. "Yes, my sweet."

"Where is she?"

"I was afraid you'd prefer her to me. And what of this princess? I've heard tell she is quite striking."

William said, "She is a child."

"She is the enemy. Have you so soon forgotten the empty stare in your father's eyes?"

"I never will." William began to move back to the camp. "No games this time, Erravane, no games... Dawn is only a few hours away. I trust your pets will harry my men no longer?"

"My dear William, they take only what they need. The disappearance of one or two in the night is of little consequence. Would you rather have them turn on me?"

For the first time as he turned back to Erravane, Adrina saw Prince William's face clearly outlined in the pale light. "Perhaps it would not be such a—"

Erravane put a finger to William's lips. "You still need me, William of Sever. Do not say a thing you will later regret." With that, Prince William strode away, and soon afterward, Erravane. Both went in separate directions.

Emel helped Adrina to her feet. Finally she took a deep releasing breath. Before she had been nearly afraid to breathe and had done so only sporadically. Erravane and William had been so close.

Adrina heard movement in the leaves behind her. She turned, sighed, knowing at once it was Valam.

"I circled around," Valam explained. "The boy?"

Adrina shrugged.

Emel who had been staring intently toward the camp said, "There, on the far side, do you see?"

Adrina and Valam turned and stared. On the opposite side of the camp, reflected in the light of the dying embers of a perimeter fire, was a mostly shadowed face. Undoubtedly, it belonged to Vilmos.

"Were you listening?" Emel asked. Valam nodded and Emel continued. "The time to make our escape is now or never."

"No," Adrina hissed angrily. "Vilmos is one of us."

Valam took Adrina's hand. "Alas, there is little we can do now.

We would waste precious time if we tried to circle the camp. We cannot. There is too much at stake. You heard as well as I, the forest is full of William's men... Perhaps it is for the best. He should fare well and, should his instincts continue to lead him south, he will find safety quickly.

"On the other hand, we will not be so fortunate. Our duty takes us north. We will have the whole of an army at our heels until we either reach Quashan' or die trying." Valam paused, took a deep breath, then added, "Quickly now..."

***

Vilmos watched his companions turn away and disappear into the gloom. Disbelief and dread flooded his thoughts. He had no idea how he had ended up on the opposite side of the camp, but *the* one thing he was sure of now was that he was on his own.

Anger quickly replaced disbelief and dread. Valam, Emel and Adrina had deserted him. Vilmos knew dawn was near and that he must act or surely he would be recaptured, but where would he run to? If he made a wide circle around the camp and tried to follow the others, could he find their trail? Did he want to find their trail? After all, they had forsaken him.

Vilmos caught movement out of the corner of his eye. He didn't wait to find out what it was he saw, he ran away fast as he could. Unsure which direction to flee, he ran aimlessly. His fear drove him on and only his instinct and the flora of the forest controlled his direction.

Then as dawn lifted darkness from the forest leaving only shadows, Vilmos stopped running. Tired, hungry and feeling desperately alone, he slumped on a moss-covered stump. He stared up through a break in the canopy where a ray of soft white light radiated down to the forest floor.

Vilmos moved to the spot bathed by the warm ray and found a sense of security in it. He thought about Prince Valam, Princess Adrina and Emel then. During his run he had come to terms with what had happened. He was no longer angry or mad at them for leaving him. He understood now that they had done what they had to do. He heard the prince's words in his ears, "… Use that chance, Vilmos, use it for all it's worth. Go back to Tabborrath Village and leave the affairs of men to men."

Suddenly Vilmos was homesick. It seemed forever since he had joined Xith and left Tabborrath Village. He lay back, crossed his arms behind his head and closed tired eyes. For a time he forgot about the dangers. He forgot that he was lost and alone in Vangar Forest. He knew only that images of home played before his closed lids.

***

With Emel leading the way and Valam pulling her, Adrina raced faster and faster. At first she gave her sore and blistered feet little thought. She flitted along, and kept pace just behind Emel.

Soon Valam was pulling her more than she moved under her own power. Soon afterward, Adrina was limping. Seemingly without thought or hesitation, Valam picked Adrina up and, with her cast her over his shoulder, continued.

For a time, all was well. Then, between her brother's gasps as he heavily sucked at the air, Adrina heard shouts from far off. Valam and Emel apparently heard them too and panic urged them to new speeds.

They raced on and on, the voices grew near intermittently and then again distant. Dawn was at hand, and gloom began to lift from the forest.

"Their trackers are worse... than those of... South Province," Emel said between breaths, "but still, what I wouldn't give for Ebony about now... He'd get the three of us... out of this accursed forest... in no time."

Valam started to laugh or so it appeared, then suddenly he doubled over, and dropped Adrina.

"It is a good time to rest," Emel said, as he slumped to the ground.

Adrina forced herself to stand on tender feet. "Are they far behind?"

"We'll know soon enough," Emel said. "Do you think you can continue on your own?"

"If you two can, I must..." Adrina was about to let her words trail off, then she decided to voice her thoughts. "Do you really think Vilmos escaped too?"

Valam stood, then turned and stared in the direction they had just come from. "Let us hope so."

Adrina's face lit with worry and showed her fears to the contrary. Emel took her hand and said, "I think he did, but now is not the time to dwell on things we cannot change."

Shortly afterward the three began running again. Adrina moved as swiftly as she could. Valam and Emel did their best to help her keep up with them. Shouts came from off to their left now and their feet lead them right. Abruptly they stumbled into a clearing. Adrina tripped over a bound and gagged figure that was lying in the grass on the edge of the clearing.

Run, said a faint voice in their minds. *Forget me. I am lost. It is a trap.*

Emel grabbed one of Adrina's hands, Valam the other. They started to race away. A circle of dark shapes with glowing eyes emerged from hiding. A voice asked, "Where are our guests going?"

Adrina recognized the voice of the speaker. "Erravane?"

Deftly the speaker stepped forward, grabbed Adrina's chin in her hand and turned her face to the pale light. "You *are* a pretty one."

Valam grabbed Erravane's arm and twisted it back as hard as he could, which brought the woman to her knees. Pain was met with sick laughter.

"Do you mock me?" Valam screamed as he twisted the arm back still further, fully expecting to hear the snap of breaking bones.

The arm began to bend and change in Valam's hand, growing thicker and shorter. Valam let go and pulled Adrina back, confusion and perhaps bewilderment showed on his face.

"If you move again," Erravane said, her voice changed as her body changed, "they will kill you."

"Close your eyes, Adrina. This is no thing for you to see," Valam shouted. "Of all the beasts of hell…"

But Adrina couldn't close her eyes, she felt compelled to watch the metamorphosis. Erravane's eyes were glowing now and fangs filled her mouth, a mouth that was twisting and contorting, growing wider and longer as Adrina look on in fascinated horror.

Valam stepped in front of Adrina protectively. "If I had my sword," Valam said, "I would run you through and send you back to the icy pits you ascended from."

Erravane snapped her head and locked powerful, wolflike jaws around Valam's hand. Screaming in agony, Valam dropped to his knees. Adrina closed her eyes and squeezed them together as tight as she could. She waited for the screaming to stop and when it did, she felt compelled to open her eyes. She was just as surprised as Valam obviously was to find he still had a hand.

Erravane, clearly no longer human, spoke with an otherworldly voice. "I said, 'no movement.'" Erravane licked her front paw.

Valam spoke again, but took care not to move. "What do you hope to gain from this? Prince William will kill the lot of you as soon as he has no need for you?"

"Ah, but I ensure that he continues to need me until I have all that I want for. And, now I have you. His precious little bargaining pieces. He will grovel on his knees to get you back."

Chapter Ten:
Conquest

The first shafts of golden light from the new day were just breaking the horizon far to the east. A wet spray blew in off the sea, and Keeper Martin shivered. He had awoken early and only he and the mid-watchmen greeted the new day.

A troubled dream had disturbed his few hours of precious sleep. Keeper Q'yer's response to his earlier dream message had been grimmer than he ever imagined it could be. Quashan' was under siege. How five hundred defenders held the city was beyond his imagining. But there had been more distressful tidings in the dream, and this, Martin didn't even want to think about.

The sound of footsteps caused Martin to turn. He eyed Captain Adylton who looked as frazzled as he felt. "You did not sleep well this night?"

"I did not sleep," answered the captain as he stared out across the dark waters.

Martin asked pointedly, "How many days to Quashan' without

the Foot?"

Captain Adylton raised an eyebrow. "Two days of hard riding, and only if we can get enough fresh horses in Alderan City. Otherwise, three at best."

"How long would it take for the Foot to catch up?"

"Foot soldiers move like sand caught in those waves," Adylton said, eyeing the frothy surf breaking against the rocks. "Depending on the weather, I'd say seven days."

"At best?"

"Six, maybe five. They'd arrive spent and—" Captain Adylton broke off, apparently he heard the footsteps as Martin did. Both men turned to see who was approaching.

"Mid-watchman," Keeper Martin said. "He's been hawking me since I stepped out here."

Captain Adylton regarded the watchman, then tossed Martin a wink. "My man... My men," he said, waving his hand in a sweeping gesture around the camp.

"And Trendmore's?"

"I gave his watchmen liberty. Told them to enjoy the Free Cities."

Keeper Martin tightened his cloak about him. "Then you've gone ahead. Are you ready?"

"Nearly so. It should all go smoothly. Better than half of his men are on liberty and he isn't the wiser... Have you received word from Alderan or has something happened in Quashan'?"

"You, Captain Adylton, are very perceptive." Martin explained about the dream message and the situation in Quashan'. Adylton grimaced. "So you see," Keeper Martin concluded, "there is precious little time to waste."

"What of Alderan? You didn't say. Did the ship arrive safely?"

Keeper Martin fixed eyes filled with distress on the captain. "Alderan is no more."

"Surely you don't mean—" Adylton began. Martin nodded solemnly. "—And, Prince Valam?"

Martin said nothing.

Martin was sure Captain Adylton was going to collapse. The captain's knees bowed and his face became ashen. Martin grabbed the captain's shoulders to steady him.

Captain Adylton turned to face the salty spray of the breaking waves. He was silent for a long time. Yet it was clear he was slowly recovering his wits as anger and finally resolve seemed to replace disbelief. "What of the sea?" Captain Adytlon asked. "We could send the foot soldiers by ship down the coast... Better still, up River Trollbridge. In autumn the rivers run high. No deep-hulled ships, but still, with the right winds and heavy oars, they could land within a day's march of Quashan'."

An incomplete smile eased Martin's downtrodden expression. "You, my friend, have never bargained with free traders. It'll take a king's ransom to pay for passage... Still, the plan is not without merit."

***

"Let me untie her. You must untie her," pleaded Adrina, "she is in obvious pain."

Do not worry unnecessarily, whispered the pleasant feminine voice in Adrina's mind. *I will journey to Great-Father, but it will not be at the hand of the likes of this.*

"Enough," snapped Erravane. "My patience is at an end. You *will* now tell me where the boy is."

The first rays of a new day pierced the thick canopy overhead, casting odd shadows about the forest floor. Erravane turned toward the light. Suddenly and swiftly, Valam lunged at Erravane, but, just as swiftly, one of Erravane's beasts leapt upon him and knocked him to the ground. Afterward, it stood defiantly upon Valam's chest, staring down at him, a deep rumbling growl escaping its throat. Adrina shuddered and edged closer to Emel.

"My pets are hungry—" Erravane reverted to human form as she spoke, her voice losing its otherworldly hue. "Do they feast on a boy or one of you? The decision is yours, but do not take too long to decide." There was anger on her face, mirrored in her eyes. She walked in a wide circle around Valam, staring down at him.

"Which will talk?" Erravane said, pointing her finger at each of the three in turn.

No one responded.

"Which will die?"

When no answer was forthcoming, Erravane said, "If you do not choose, then I will choose." With a lightning fast snap of her wrists, Erravane wrapped her hands around Adrina's throat. "I choose the princess."

Adrina recoiled, the hands tensed around her throat until it seemed she could not breathe. Terrified, Adrina stared wildly at Erravane. Beside her Valam and Emel attempted to gain to their feet, but one of the Wolmerrelle had likewise leapt upon Emel.

"Why do you care so about a boy?" Adrina asked, her words coming out through a strained gasp. "Vilmos is long gone."

"His *name*," Erravane said sinisterly. "Thank you. Now, where did he go?"

"Home, for all we know."

Erravane tightened her grip on Adrina's throat. Her long, sharp fingernails pierced the skin and drew blood. "That is not the answer I want. I tire of this, and I too hunger for a feast."

Straining ineffectively to raise his chest under the weight of the Wolmerrelle, Emel craned his head upward. "Let Adrina go! I will die willingly in her stead."

Erravane started to laugh, a deep demented cackle. "So noble, so very noble. What about you Prince of the North? Would you die for her too?"

Valam said, "Let them both go and I will do whatever it is you ask."

"Is that a promise?"

"Stop!" shouted a voice vaguely familiar to Adrina. "You do not know what it is you do. Make no promises to her kind." Xith emerged from the shadows and stood with his hands extended before Erravane.

"Watcher," Erravane said, no surprise in her voice. "Age takes your stealth. You clomp around like a Man. I wondered what it would take to make you reveal yourself, and now I know."

"This is *no game*. What is occurring is of *no concern* to you." Xith's eyes glowed as he regarded Adrina momentarily. Adrina saw strange emotions on his face and there was a quality in his voice that escaped her ears. "*Return to Ril Akh Arr and Under-Earth,* Erravane."

Erravane hissed, then attacked Xith. She knocked him down

and stood over him. Xith made no move to defend himself.

"Attempt your guile of Voice on me again," Erravane said, "and I will kill you."

"Then kill me, Erravane, I grow weary."

Erravane hissed again and released Xith's throat. "You sicken me. All of you sicken me. So willing to die. So willing to sacrifice. Is the will to survive in any of you?"

Erravane cocked her head as if listening to the wind. "You are too late Watcher. The hunt is joined. Oh, they are joyous!"

"Vilmos did not kill Rake. It was I who took his head."

Erravane laughed again, the same sickly cackle. "I know, which is why I will enjoy their feast all the more."

"Return to your forests. Nothing that happens here concerns your kind. You tamper with forces you do not understand."

"I will leave in good time, once I have what I came for."

"And what is that?" Xith asked.

Adrina shouted, "Prince William!"

Xith jumped to his feet. "Is that it, Erravane?... Your appetite has changed."

"I already have his child in my womb."

Xith laughed. "If you had so precious a cargo you would have returned to Ril Akh Arr... A half-breed child of royal blood no less..." Xith added the Voice at the last, "*Let Vilmos go. You do not need him.*"

Erravane pounced on Xith and slashed his face with her fingernails. "I warned you, Watcher. I *will* kill the boy now."

As if stung, Xith reeled away from Erravane. "And if he kills your pets, what then? What will you do then?"

"He will not."

"What if? What then? Would you no longer meddle in affairs that do not concern you?"

Erravane was obviously irritated at the course of the conversation. "Yes," she shot back at Xith.

"Is that a promise?"

"And if the boy dies, what then?"

Xith said simply, "I will surrender to your will."

"I would have you surrender regardless."

"You are far from our realm, further still from the forest temple of Arr. Attempt a test of wills here and you will lose." Erravane slashed Xith across the face again. Xith held his ground. "If Vilmos survives, you will return to Under-Earth. If he dies, I will do as you bid. I would even help you birth the child if that is your wish."

Erravane's eyes widened greedily. "You would birth an abomination?"

Xith slowly nodded.

Erravane grinned. "Your faith in a human child will be your undoing."

***

Quite sure what had awoken him, Vilmos stirred. He had been dreaming of Tabborrath Village but thoughts and dreams all spun away. His eyes were wide, his mind in shock. From not far off came another long wailing cry, joined by more, which were still distant. Vilmos had sudden flashbacks to another time in Vangar Forest. He knew with certainty the Wolmerrelle hunted him.

He cast aside the prince's overtunic. The oversized garment

had kept him warm during these past dreary days and chilly nights. Now he needed speed and not warmth.

Then as he started to flee, he caught a bit of an old memory. Perhaps he could trick the Wolmerrelle just as he knew he could the hounds of Tabborrath's huntmaster. Without delay, Vilmos retrieved the tunic. He dragged it along the ground, then scrambled up into a nearby tree and left the tunic there.

Then Vilmos ran. He had no idea where he ran to, only that he ran away from the howls. The boughs of trees passed as dark blurs around him and as he ran, Vilmos imagined that Xith was beside him and that the shaman urged him to race faster and faster.

They lead us, whispered an old voice in his mind. Vilmos nodded in understanding. He veered right instead of left where the unnerving calls sought to lead him.

His race became a race of desperation. He ran to escape, only to escape. On and on he raced. He used his hands to ward off branches that seemed to reach out to grab him as he passed. He mounted a rise and started down its backside. There, he found his second wind. The path muddied at the bottom of the rise. He came to a stream, kneeled briefly to drink of its cool waters, then hurried on. The calls were never far off.

Completely winded, Vilmos stopped. Clutching his chest, panting for air, he hunched over. His face, cold despite the perspiration that dripped from his brow, stung where branches had caught his cheeks. He fought to get his breathing under control and bit back the pain of sore muscles.

Gradually the splotches before his eyes cleared and he brought his breathing under control. He straightened up and looked around, noticing then that the forest seemed suddenly too quiet. His face blank and expressionless, Vilmos panned his eyes slowly from left to right.

Out of the corner of his eye, he caught movement and perhaps, a flash of white. Suddenly, the voice of the past was in his mind again, *From this lesson stems the basis of your magical shield, the shield that will protect and keep you in dangerous times...*

Vilmos conjured the magical shield now, just as he had then. Out of the corner of his eye, he watched a great black blur sweep toward him. A yelp followed as the creature struck the invisible barrier. Still, its momentum carried Vilmos to the ground with it.

Disoriented, Vilmos shook his head and inhaled. The force of the blow had knocked the wind out of him. For an instant, it was as if Vilmos didn't think at all. All his bewildered thoughts stopped, the magical shield fell away, and then the beast howled and struck again.

Vilmos struck back with his fists. He clubbed the side of one of the Wolmerrelle's two heads. The creature wheeled back. Vilmos crab-crawled backwards as fast as he could. Only his back slamming against the trunk of a tree stopped his crazed retreat. Then without even realizing what he was doing, a trace of blue-white light danced across his fingertips. The bolt raced outward and caught the Wolmerrelle full in the torso. Howling madly, it staggered backward.

Vilmos pressed his back against the tree trunk, and, using his knees, inched up to a standing position. Still, he was terrified and his every thought screamed out to him, Escape! Again magic raced from his hands and struck the howling Wolmerrelle. The smell of singed fur and flesh choked the air. The creature charged, but managed only a single stride before collapsing.

For the longest time Vilmos didn't move. He sat wide-eyed, his thoughts still racing, still screaming, Run! Escape! Get away! But the Wolmerrelle was no longer moving.

Cautiously, Vilmos crept forward. He reached out with his foot and nudged the beast. He jumped back as it convulsed. Then, it moved no more.

Vilmos was elated, tired from his flight and drained from the brief fight. He collapsed to his haunches, but was given little time to recover. A glimmer of movement out of the corner of his vision caught his eye. Suddenly he knew more of the creatures lurked just beyond his view in the shadows. He raised the magical shield. Again it saved him. Only this time the great beast did not carry Vilmos to the ground with it, and this time he maintained the shield.

They came at him then, one by one in a great wave. Vilmos struggled to maintain the shield and keep his feet. Magic surged wildly through him as he drew in more and more energy. Consumed by it, Vilmos turned wild eyes on the five Wolmerrelle that circled him, waiting to pounce.

Again Vilmos' thoughts were propelled to the past. In his mind as he poised for the attack and turned in a tight circle, it was the great black bear that he saw. Reared up on its hind legs, it towered over him, a mountain of black fur and dark eyes.

Vilmos was no longer gripped by terror as he stared up at it. The voice in his mind no longer screamed, RUN! It was chastising him. *Control! Always stay in control,* it said.

Vilmos fought to gain control of the rampant energies within him. Perhaps sensing a moment of weakness, the Wolmerrelle charged.

Vilmos' shield held them at bay and the charge served to focus his thoughts. Suddenly he realized something. Xith had traveled through Vangar Forest to reach the clearing beyond his village. He had all but admitted it. He had arrived on horseback and no horse could have descended into the valley from anywhere within many miles of that clearing. And that night when Midori had left the camp, she had taken the horse with her, for the animal hadn't been there the next morning.

Vilmos' own voice rang in his ears, *You weren't expecting hunters and trackers were you. Who were you expecting shaman?*

There is no need to trouble over the could have beens, returned Xith's voice, and Vilmos was now sure that the great black bear hadn't mauled and killed the girl from Olex Village. The bear hadn't attacked him during that fateful encounter and it probably wouldn't have. Evident anger in his eyes and on his face, Vilmos turned to face the first of the great two-headed beasts.

Do what you must… rang Xith's voice in his ears.

The urge to let the magic flow unchecked through him was suddenly strong. Vilmos fought to control it and instead channeled that strength carefully to his hands. Bolts of blue-white lightening sprang forth and struck one of the beasts. The creature died.

Vilmos' magical shield fell as the remaining four attacked and overwhelmed him. White-hot fire shot through his right leg as a pair of powerful jaws clamped down on it. Vilmos let out a scream that shook the trees and rang through the forest.

Pain flooded his thoughts, panic took over. Wildly Vilmos lashed out again and again, wielding his magic, punching, even kicking when necessary to fend off the relentless beasts.

Again, he found himself with his back to the trunk of one of the great trees of the forest. The last of the great beasts stared him down. Vilmos could barely stand now, and only the tree at his back kept him on his feet. Too weary to focus, too weary to find his center, he knew only that the magic was gone now, gone with his rage.

Vilmos didn't think it odd that this beast had only one head, though he did take note of it. This Wolmerrelle was smaller than the others, still somehow more powerful. Its eyes, glowing even in the light of the new day, regarded him in an almost human way. Though badly wounded, it dragged its hind legs while howling a tormented wail up at the heavens and came at him.

In an attempt to flee, Vilmos stumbled and fell. The injured leg that had held him while his fervor raged, collapsed under his weight. Vilmos' face slapped the hard earth first, his hands were too slow to brace against the fall. With his face pressed against wet earth, muddied with blood surely his own as well as the fallen beasts, Vilmos lay where he fell, too drained to move.

A shadow blocked out the daylight filtering in through the forest canopy. Vilmos rolled his eyes up to see the Wolmerrelle standing over him. He shielded his face with his arms as it set upon him. The creature latched onto the arm and shook its head wildly.

Vilmos groped frantically with his free hand and kicked at the beast's head with his one good leg. His hand found only leaves and dirt, but there was something on the ground just outside his reach.

He could feel the edge of it. *Shape your power, use it to your advantage! Concentrate, control, focus!* screamed the voice in his mind. Vilmos squeezed his eyes tight, fighting the pain, fighting to concentrate.

He focused on the object just out of his reach. It was the clubbed end of broken branch, he could feel it now vibrating on the ground. It wanted to inch forward into his grasp. Then suddenly it was in his hand and Vilmos began bludgeoning the beast.

The weakened Wolmerrelle howled and hissed. Repeatedly, it raked Vilmos' chest with its forepaws. For an instant as he beat with all his might on the creature's head, Vilmos swore he saw a human face—his weary mind and body were surely playing tricks on him. He mustered the strength to deliver a last desperate blow and then dealt it, putting every bit of himself into the blow. The crunching sound of bone and wood followed. The branch broke. The beast collapsed and just as suddenly as the attack had come it was over.

Blood covered Vilmos' face. His hands. His arms. He knew not whether it was his own. He didn't care. He had won.

"I did it," Vilmos whispered to the voice in his mind. *You performed excellently,* the voice whispered back. Vilmos managed a smile. Then, weak from blood loss and battle, he collapsed.

***

"If you strike," Xith said, regarding the clawed hand raised to his throat, "know that our arrangement is void. In addition, if you do not kill me with that single blow, know that I *will* kill you. Know also that the boy's powers pale in comparison to my own and that my memory is as long as time itself. One day I *will* return to Under-

Earth. It is in your hands whether I make my life's last work the siege of Ril Akh Arr or other matters…"

Deftly Erravane swept back her hand. "This is far from over." She said it evilly. She was hiding something and apparently Xith knew it.

"If you have designs on Prince William, think again. I need him alive."

"So do I," hissed Erravane.

"It is over, Erravane!" Xith grabbed Erravane's throat with a mystical force that Adrina couldn't see but knew was there. Erravane's beasts raced to her aid but crashed against an invisible barrier. Viciously they attacked the unseen wall but couldn't break through.

"Do not dismiss me," hissed Erravane despite the pressure of the phantom's grasp on her throat. A dozen more Wolmerrelle emerged from the shadows and suddenly the woods were full of long wailing cries. "You kill me and you will never leave the forest alive."

Xith pointed his finger at one of Erravane's beasts. A line of fire raced from his hand and engulfed it.

Adrina gasped. She realized the source of Xith's mysterious powers. "Forbidden magic," she whispered.

Erravane screamed a tortured wail that matched the dying Wolmerrelle's. Her face twisted and contorted as she sought to change shapes, but no matter what she did, she couldn't break free of the phantom's grasp.

A figure emerged from the shadows. Deep blue eyes looked in Adrina's direction momentarily, then suddenly the figure was moving with inhuman speed among the pack of Wolmerrelle. "Seth," whispered Adrina. The still figure whose head Adrina held answered, *Yes,* and there was evident relief in the tone.

Xith matched Seth's blows one for one with a stinging magical flame. One by one the Wolmerrelle fell. Eyes bulging, Erravane clawed at the air and before Emel and Prince Valam could gain their feet and join the fray, she cried out, "Enough, enough. Stop!"

Mid-blow Seth stopped, drew up to his full height and cast a sidelong glance at Erravane. The remaining Wolmerrelle made no move to attack him. Dumbfounded, Emel and Valam looked to Xith.

"It is over," Xith said. "If *you* leave here alive, Erravane, it will be up to you... Cease struggling, the grip will be relaxed accordingly." Erravane hissed but ceased to struggle against the unseen phantom. Xith turned to Adrina then, "Ease your fears Princess, those creatures cannot break through."

Xith then turned to Seth. "You are bleeding."

It is only a scratch.

"As superficial as that single scratch may seem, it could kill you if not cleaned properly. Untreated, it will fester like nothing you have ever seen." He paused, then turned back to Adrina, "I must apologize for waiting so long, but I had to be sure—"

"What of our deal?" interrupted Erravane, "You promised I'd go free."

"I made no such promise, though you did promise to return to Ril Akh Arr and meddle no longer in affairs that do not concern you or your kind."

Adrina broke her trancelike gaze on Xith. She looked once

more to pitiful Erravane, then beckoned to Seth. "Sit beside me," she said, "let me clean your wound."

Xith smiled fondly at Adrina, as if remembering a thing from the past. Then he turned back to Erravane, who had begun to howl.

"Let me go," Erravane hissed, "you have what you wanted."

Xith forced the phantom's grip. "Answer this question with care, your life depends on it. When will William meet King Jarom?"

"I do not know… You must let me go."

"She lies," Emel said. "Adrina and I overheard her speaking to Prince William. His commanders will join him at his camp tomorrow."

Erravane cringed and cowered away from Xith's stare. She began babbling. "His army is ready to march. The encampments are spread out all along the northern edge of the forest. William awaits the arrival of King Jarom's army before he strikes. King Jarom's advanced guard has already struck against Quashan', they lay siege to the city days ago."

"Where is Jarom's army now?" questioned Xith. "Where is King Jarom?"

"Quashan', but the bulk of his army has just entered the southern edge of the Vangar. Even with the paths cut by William's path forgers, days will pass before they arrive."

The unseen hand lifted Erravane off her feet. Xith asked, "William doesn't know this?"

"He knows only what I see fit to tell him."

Momentarily, Adrina saw surprise or perhaps glee cross Xith's face. Xith said, "The games end, Erravane. I would sooner cut out your tongue than listen to you speak. If you lie about King Jarom, I will kill you now and be done with it."

"He is an overzealous man who thinks he cannot lose. My beasts took great pleasure in harrying his soldiers... They are truly afraid of these forests now."

Xith seemed pleased with the answer. "You are free to go Erravane. Know that I make no empty promises. If ever I see you again, I will kill you, and more... Return to Under-Earth for it is there that you belong, and not here."

The expression in Erravane's eyes as the unseen hand released her, matched that which had been in Xith's eyes moments earlier. Adrina and the others watched as Erravane and her beasts slipped away into the shadows. As Adrina had finished cleaning his wound, Seth now saw to Galan's needs. He held a water bag to Galan's lips and she drank heavily.

Emel spoke first, voicing the thoughts also on Adrina's mind. "Do you really believe Erravane will do as you asked? I don't trust her."

Neither do I, sent Seth.

"Though eventually she will keep her promise, Erravane is hardly one to be taken at her word. She is strong willed and wants what it is she came for, this I am counting on." Xith turned to Galan and Seth, "Can she walk unaided?"

Alas no, Brother Galan is weak from thirst and hunger...

Valam, who had been quietly regarding Galan's lithe figure, said, "I will carry her." Adrina had never seen such a look in her brother's eyes. Valam was smitten by Galan's angelic beauty, or so it appeared.

"Good, good," Xith said. "We have little more than this day and the next to set matters straight... But first we must find Vilmos."

Adrina turned to Xith. "I must ask," she said. "Where have you been these many past days? Where is Father Jacob?"

"Know that this way matters have turned out better than they otherwise would have. I had very important matters to attend to, and I am truly sorry if you feel that I abandoned you when you needed me the most."

"What of Father Jacob?"

"Jacob is well, but surely irritated," was all Xith said.

Chapter Eleven:
Full Circle

"Well met, Keeper Q'yer. What brings you to the walls?" asked Sergeant Danyel'.

"A dream," responded the keeper, his voice distant, his eyes searching the horizon.

Sergeant Danyel' turned about on his heel and looked out at the campfires that dotted the landscape like a swarm of lightning bugs. "At dawn they will come again. They attack alternately from the south, east and west, leaving only the north wall alone. They toy with us and keep us occupied though I know not why. Perhaps Great-Father truly smiles upon us, for if they ever once attacked in full force, we would be swept away."

Danyel's voice became soft. "What I would not give for a spy among them."

Keeper Q'yer seemed to only half listen to Danyel' as he stared, then as he turned away he asked, "What of Chancellor Van'te?"

"He sleeps awaiting the attack. I beg you not to disturb him if it is your plan. It is the first he's slept in days. We need his direction tomorrow."

"I bring good news, I think he would approve."

Danyel' regarded the keeper's troubled eyes. "You don't look like a man bearing good news."

"With the good there is always the bad. Will I find the chancellor in his quarters?"

"No, he has taken up residence elsewhere. I will take you to him if I must."

"You must, this is important, a dream message from Keeper Martin."

***

Adrina drove her mount still faster. She tried to shake images of the boy from her mind. They had found Vilmos lying on ground saturated with blood some hours after Erravane had disappeared into the forest shadows. Adrina was certain that death had found him by now and tried to convince herself that perhaps Vilmos had found peace.

She cast the thoughts away and whipped the reins of her mount. She glanced to Emel and Valam who rode in tight formation on either side of her. She couldn't help noting the defiant pride in Emel's eyes as he stroked his Ebony. How Xith had safeguarded and kept their horses after Alderan was beyond her.

To Adrina it was clear that Emel was both excited and troubled. The reunion between master and mount had been a sweet one and left Adrina a bit envious. Emel had not hid his joy at the sight of his beloved steed.

It was now well into the afternoon. The three had left the southern forests in early morning. Slipping through William's lines had been easier than Adrina imagined it would be. One thing was clear, the soldiers weren't expecting anyone to pass through their ranks. Their camps had no guards posted forward or rear.

An enemy army, worse, an enemy army without cares, so close to Kingdom soil, had outraged them all. Valam, seemingly the most. More than once Adrina had watched him fight back the urge to charge into one of the sleepy camps and slaughter the unwary louts—"louts" being Valam's word for them.

As they neared the top of a small rise, Valam signaled a halt. Adrina reined in her mount and dismounted. "Dusk is still a few hours away," she said. "Why do we stop?"

Valam, clearly deep in thought and already preparing to rub down his mount's tired legs, didn't seem to hear Adrina's question.

Emel said, "We can't afford a lame mount now, Adrina, despite our urge to race on. I'll rub down Ebony and if you'll walk him after, I'll do your mount."

"I'll rub down my own horse. Show me what I must do."

"You should rest. His Highness may wish to press on through the night and we will surely end up walking at some point."

"Do you speak for my brother now?"

Emel cast her a glum stare then turned back to Ebony. He removed Ebony's saddle and walked him for a time, then began using a comb from his saddlebags. Imitating his actions, Adrina did her best to rub down her steed. Never had she imagined that rubbing down an animal could be so tiring.

Afterward she found she had to rinse the stink of animal sweat from her hands. Exhausted, Adrina sat cross-legged and unladylike upon the ground. Days of captivity and hardship had nearly numbed her awareness to proper mannerisms, and it was only absently that she felt the moisture of the tall grasses.

As a voice from the past flashed through her mind, Adrina looked to Valam who was stretched out on the ground and staring up at the darkening sky. She knew that though he looked relaxed, he was brooding. "I miss you, Lady Isador," Adrina whispered to the fleeting voice in her mind, "perhaps you were right, wintering with Rudden Klaiveson wouldn't have been so bad a thing."

Adrina found Emel's eyes upon her. "I didn't mean to snap at you."

"I know."

"Is there really hope in this race? I mean, Quashan' is east, we ride north and we haven't even crossed the river—"

"His Highness knows what he is doing. There is a ford nearby, we will cross it and then follow the far branch of the river back to the south and east."

"What did he and Xith talk about? They spoke at length. Valam said nothing and we've been riding all day. Neither of you have said anything, what am I supposed to think?"

Suddenly Adrina noticed Valam was on his feet. Valam said, "You yourself saw William's army in the forest. You know that the entirety of the second most powerful army in all the lands marches north and that Quashan' is under siege. What is there to say?"

Adrina cast imploring eyes in Valam's direction.

"This is no place for you, Adrina. Why father ever let you leave Imtal when he was aware of the troubles here, I'll never understand. And why Keeper Martin and Father Jacob let you continue the journey when they knew there was danger is a matter I intend to take up—"

Emel put his hand on Valam's shoulder. Valam regarded it but still continued, "These are things that must be said, things I could not find heart to say before. But now that we are clear of danger for a time, I must speak my mind."

"No one is to blame but me, Valam. You know I get what I want—it has always been that way. If you're going to point the finger at anyone, point it at me."

"There will be time for blame and arguments later," Emel said, "with luck we will be upon the road to Quashan' in the morning."

A deep worry was written on Valam's face as he turned away from Adrina and said to Emel, "It is a hope, yes."

***

"You want me to what?" screamed the galley's captain above the sound of pace keeper's drums.

"I want you to continue up river," said Keeper Martin.

"Captain Adylton, you claim to be a fisher's son, bring some sense to your companion."

Captain Adylton had been watching the rise and fall of the sweeps as they stroked the water and it took him a moment to respond. "If any of your ships are damaged, we'll pay you double its worth in gold from the King's treasury."

"Night is nigh at hand."

"Triple," said Adylton.

The ship captain still seemed hesitant.

Captain Adylton said, "Plus a year's wages for lost revenues during rebuilding."

"Lanterns!" shouted the galley captain, "Bow, starboard, port. Close watch! Drummer, mid beat! Relay the orders to the rest of the fleet!"

Keeper Martin nodded approval. He and Captain Adylton moved away from the helm so their voices wouldn't be within earshot of the galley's captain. With the noise of the drums, the grunts of the rowers and the splash of the sweeps, they didn't have to go far.

Keeper Martin said, "You learn the ways of free traders quickly."

"I didn't say I'd never bargained with free traders before, my friend, what I said was 'I disliked free traders.' Yet I suppose there are worse ills in the world than a hunger for gold."

"Well said, but how much is it going to cost to convince him to continue when one of his precious ships really hits bottom?"

Captain Adylton frowned. "Do you believe the river still so shallow, even with the recent rains?"

"If the Trollbridge was safely traversable at any time during the year, an enterprising captain, perhaps even our ship's captain, would've been sailing it long ago, and there would be ports up and down—"

"—I get the point," Captain Adylton said, shifting his stance as the boat swayed. "We will pray then that none of his ships run aground." Captain Adylton tried to change the topic of the conversation. "Did this Keeper Q'yer of yours receive your message yet?"

"The message entered Keeper Q'yer's dreams as I sent it, that is the way of the message. What I don't know is if he understood it, though we will surely find out soon enough."

***

Father Jacob eyed the grizzled commander who stood beside him. Reflecting the light of the new day, his brown eyes shone with an uncanny luster. There was naked rage on his face; he was gritting his teeth and his hand on Jacob's shoulder was trying to crush bone. Then, his tone grim, Captain Mikhal said, "A costly attack at dawn it will be, but we must strike now. I cannot bare the sight of this."

Jacob peered out from his hiding place amidst the trees. From his vantage point, he saw most of Quashan' and the amassed army. The emblems on the enemy banners at this distance were hardly identifiable, though the colors were. They were not green and gold, but blue and black. The colors of King Jarom and the Kingdom of Vostok. Jacob bowed his head wearily, but didn't respond.

The two stood there for a time, staring down at the army poised to strike the city as they obviously had in previous days. Quashan's walls were battered. The east wall, which they had the best view of, had large sections missing from its upper bulwarks. Thin trails of black smoke were streaming from the southern part of the city and a section of the nearby wall was charred.

Captain Mikhal turned and started to walk away. Father Jacob stopped him. "I too am nearly at the end of my patience. For days I have done nothing but wait, and while I grow tired of waiting, I made a promise to an old friend that I would wait when it seemed we must attack and he in turn made a promise to me."

"There are exceptions to any promise, and this is surely one, unless this friend of yours is His Royal Majesty or My Lord Prince or—"

"Who he is not important, that I trust him and would give my life for his *is* important. No, we must wait."

Captain Mikhal hissed and cursed in a low voice. He pointed, then spoke, "Look, ridesman, lancers. Hundreds."

"White and red," Jacob said quietly.

Captain Mikhal regarded Jacob. "It cannot be, it doesn't make sense."

Jacob sighed and bowed his head wearily. "Prince William's advance guard, his army comes."

"But, the Alliance?"

"The Alliance died with King Charles."

Captain Mikhal's nostrils flared. "That is as impossible as—"

"—an order sealed with King Andrew's seal rousing the whole of Quashan' garrison to Imtal being false?"

Before Captain Mikhal could respond, Father Jacob explained the last thing he had been holding back from the garrison commander. He spoke quickly and directly, telling Captain Mikhal a thing that he himself had not wanted to believe until he saw it with his own eyes. "The Kingdom of Vostok and the Kingdom of Sever are united in their cause against Great Kingdom."

"If the Alliance is broken, what of Zapad and Yug? King Peter and King Alexas are marionettes, and King Jarom is the puppeteer."

"We must give thanks to Mother-Earth and her divine providence."

"Even the Stygian Palisades have passes, and there are certainly enough ships in the Far…" Seeming to realize what he was saying, Captain Mikhal's voice trailed off.

Suddenly the call of dozens of trumpets broke the air.

Captain Mikhal's face was livid as he said, "They're preparing an assault. The time to strike is now while they muster. Nothing you say will make me change my mind. Nothing."

"Who will you serve by charging to your deaths? You must trust in—"

"—I've little faith, Father Jacob, I must confess this, for if you are going to tell me that I must trust in Great-Father, you'll find me lacking."

Father Jacob put his hand on Captain Mikhal's shoulder. "I have faith for the both of us. I was about to say that you must trust in me."

Jacob paused and took a deep breath. He was about to speak when more trumpet calls broke the silence.

"The attack begins," said Captain Mikhal, his hand returned to Jacob's shoulder was again trying to crush bone. "My hand yearns for the hilt of my blade, can you know what it does to me to see this?"

Jacob winced. "Yes, I do know."

"We strike," Captain Mikhal said, "we strike."

***

In the middle of a circle of trees they sat. Seth beside Galan. Vilmos opposite Xith and the mysterious lady.

Vilmos listened carefully to the tall light-haired woman who he was sure had saved his life when no other could have. Mid-sentence she had turned to him and Vilmos knew she was now speaking to him. He wondered if she had read his thoughts.

"—like a tree with many limbs that branch out forever. With each new branch comes a choice and for right or wrong you follow one or the other." The lady paused, then stood. "Sometimes, two great boughs touch and, for a time, their branches intertwine. Sometimes, the great trees form a circle such as this."

She gestured to the circle of trees. "And, for good or evil, they form an ever continuing chain. The evil that plays upon the hearts and minds of the disenchanted has its part in the chain. You cannot cleanse yourself of it forever, though you can hold it in check. You, Vilmos, have found yourself. Do not lose or waste what you have gained."

The lady turned to Xith. "Go with my blessing. Remember, you will find help in a most unlikely source. And, to Quashan' you hasten—" She looked at the others each in turn. "—Galan, Seth, Vilmos, remember what I have told you. Sometimes it is best to remember our roots, for a tree without roots cannot grow."

She stood and Xith bowed his head. Seth and Galan did likewise and then Vilmos. Vilmos had only just looked down—for an instant, no more—but when he glanced up, the lady was gone. He flashed excited eyes to Xith, suddenly realizing something else. *The trees were gone?*

Vilmos felt emotions flood over him—first surprise, then alarm—a chill ran up his back. He looked to Galan and Seth—to him, their abilities were both strange and wonderful. He turned then to see what they saw. He was on a hillside, there was a walled city in the distance. However, the sun virging in the East shrouded all detail in a golden haze. Faintly, he heard what could have been trumpet calls.

"There is much to be done before this day is finished," Xith said, waving for Vilmos, Seth and Galan to follow him. "I pray that we are not too late and that Father Jacob still waits."

***

Sergeant Danyel' burst into Chancellor Van'te's chamber. "The attack comes, we must hasten to the walls!"

Chancellor Van'te looked to Keeper Q'yer and when neither spoke, Danyel' repeated, "We must hasten to the walls."

Chancellor Van'te stood then and as he did, he again looked to Keeper Q'yer. Keeper Q'yer raised a hand to his lips. Instead of responding, Chancellor Van'te indicated Danyel' should lead the way.

As Danyel' turned to enter the hall, a runner, panting and out of breath, appeared in the doorway. "Hurry, the enemy…"

The runner paused to inhale and to wipe sweat from his forehead.

"We know," Danyel' said, wiping sweat and grime from his own brow.

Danyel' stumbled as he took a step toward the runner. Van'te grabbed his arm to steady him.

The runner continued, "No, you don't understand…"

Danyel' said, "Go on."

Chancellor Van'te looked to Keeper Q'yer again. He already knew what the runner would say, still, he listened.

"They come from the south… the east, and the… west in a great swarm."

Sergeant Danyel's face turned ashen. Chancellor Van'te

steadied him as he nearly fell, then handed him off to Keeper Q'yer. "He is the one who has not slept since the siege began. Take care of him. I'll go do what I can.

"And keeper—" Chancellor Van'te stared directly into Keeper Q'yer's eyes. "—I pray that no more of what you've told me comes true."

Chapter Twelve:
Battle

Vilmos saw Captain Mikhal glance toward the city then heavenward. From the direction of the city came the sounds of a raging battle. It was midmorning, only two hours after they had found Father Jacob, and things looked surely grim for the defenders. Smoke was rising from the eastern part of the city as well as the southern part now.

"They'll come. *Patience,* Captain Mikhal," Xith said.

Captain Mikhal fixed eyes filled with rage on Xith. "No more, your promises are empty. For the life of me, I don't understand why I listened to—"

"Please," Father Jacob said, "don't you see the folly in such a pointless attack? Only united with the soldiers of Imtal do we have a chance."

"I see only that the defenders will soon be overwhelmed. The Quashan' garrison isn't the largest in the Kingdom, isn't the strongest, isn't the best equipped, but we'll be damned if we stand by and watch our homes destroyed. Never underestimate the determination of men defending their homes. We'll fight. We'll fight like demons possessed."

"You should *relax*," Xith said.

Father Jacob said, "I pray that you will listen to reason."

"Save your prayers for the enemy when we drive them from our lands. The burning in my heart is matched two-thousand fold by the burning in the hearts of my soldiers. We fight."

Before Jacob or Xith could respond, Captain Mikhal turned about on his heel in military fashion, and strode away.

Xith stopped Jacob from going after him. "You cannot change the minds of those who are already convinced to the contrary."

Captain Mikhal didn't waste any time, already he was barking orders to his men. Vilmos didn't know military tactics, still, it was clear Captain Mikhal did. Vilmos was about to speak when a masculine voice sounded in his mind.

He deems himself a failure. He will charge to his death if you let him.

"I know," Xith said. "Can you ride?"

Seth sent an odd sensation of warmth that Vilmos had slowly come to realize meant a curt yes.

Xith motioned to an attendant and indicated the man should bring three horses. Xith said, "Brother Galan, watch well young Vilmos. He is an apt apprentice, and I shouldn't like to see him do anything that will sever our relationship prematurely."

At the hearing, Vilmos smiled. Xith had expressed genuine feelings for him. Then when he realized Xith aimed to race off without him, Vilmos frowned.

Before Vilmos could voice an objection, Xith said, "A very

important task falls to you, Vilmos and Galan. You must go up into the highlands, then circle west until you can see Quashan's west gatehouse. There you must await the arrival of His Highness, Prince of Great Kingdom. Explain the situation to him as you know it." Xith looked directly at Vilmos. "Remember what I said about Erravane."

Xith paused and cast a sidelong glance to Captain Mikhal. A runner had just returned. "Captain," the runner said, "the sub-commander of the Foot awaits your orders."

Captain Mikhal nodded to the sub-commander of the Horse who was beside him. The sub-commander came to attention then departed. Captain Mikhal went off in the opposite direction.

Just then, attendants returned with the horses. Xith, Seth and Father Jacob mounted. It seemed Xith was going to say something more, but then Captain Mikhal ordered his foot soldiers to begin their advance. The three squadrons of foot soldiers, some fifteen hundred men, began their charge. They burst from the forest and raced down the slopes that they knew so well, into the Quashan' valley basin, using the contours of the land to hide their movement as best as they could.

Meanwhile, the horse soldiers waited. Captain Mikhal had divided the Horse into two files. One would later sweep in along the northern flank of the Foot, the other the southern, but only when the time was right, for Captain Mikhal hoped the Foot would cover considerably more than half the distance to the city before the enemy would spot them and turn about to set up a rear defense. Only then would the Horse begin their charge.

Captain Mikhal's stallion pranced anxiously as the captain held the animal's reins taut. Xith, Seth and Father Jacob, on horseback, were beside him now. Captain Mikhal reached into his saddlebag and handed each a strip of green and gold cloth. "Field insignia," Vilmos heard the captain say, "tie it around your right arm. Do not lose it, it is the only thing that will identify you with the Kingdom forces in the mayhem to come. Father Jacob, stay close, I will do my best to protect you, for we will surely have need of your healing abilities."

"Would that I were a priestess," muttered Jacob.

From high overhead, Vilmos heard the call of an eagle. He looked up, and saw it circling above the city. He looked to Xith. The shaman's eyes were glossed over.

The Foot was nearly halfway across the valley floor. Vilmos expected at any time to see the enemy host turn to form a defense. But they didn't. And the Foot continued their silent race.

Vilmos glanced to Xith again, then back down the hillside. He looked beyond the Kingdom foot soldiers to the great walled city of Quashan'. He couldn't see the men upon the walls, though he knew they were there. They were the ones pushing back the breaching ladders and responding to the enemy's relentless charges with catapult volleys.

Suddenly the eagle dove from the heavens and just when it seemed it would crash into the walls of the city, it disappeared. Xith came out of his trance and said something to Captain Mikhal that Vilmos couldn't hear. Captain Mikhal raised his sword arm high overhead, momentarily his broad-bladed sword glistened in the late morning sun, then he thrust the blade forward. The charge began. More than five hundred riders spurred their mounts into a race.

Vilmos stood enthralled, unable to break away. The thunder of hooves blocked out the sounds of the distant battle. Galan at his side was silent. She too watched and listened. Eventually though, the thunder grew distant. The first excited shouts erupted from the enemy host and men scrambled to set up a frenzied rear defense.

Midway down the valley's slopes now, the Kingdom horse soldiers spurred their mounts, driving the animals as fast as they dared. Arrows from the Kingdom bowmen began to penetrate the enemy lines and soon afterward the first wave of foot soldiers struck the enemy's rear flank. Privately, Vilmos cheered for the Kingdomers, but he was also torn between loyalties. Some of those on the field were from his homeland.

As Vilmos watched, Sever's Knights of the Lance, their red and white banners waving in the wind, rallied for a clash with the Kingdom riders. Instead of turning to engage them, Captain Mikhal's horse soldiers continued directly into the enemy ranks. Even from this distance, Vilmos heard the screams of despair, agony and panic that followed.

It is time, imparted Galan into Vilmos' mind. *We have a long walk ahead.*

***

Captain Mikhal's mount reared up on its hind legs. All around the captain was the press of enemy soldiers. He removed his foot from the stirrup, kicked out an approaching soldier. The heel of his boot struck the side of the man's skull. Abruptly the soldier stopped, his knees crumbled under his weight. Captain Mikhal didn't pause. He turned his mount, struck down with his long blade, and like a cleaver, it hew a defender before him. Captain Mikhal continued his charge.

Xith tried to stay close to Captain Mikhal. He defended himself as best as he could, relying largely on his magic shield while he concentrated on other matters. There was a breach midway along Quashan's east wall and in just a few seconds as he watched, dozens of attackers had pushed their way up onto the wall. There they were carving out an ever-growing section. At the base of the wall, many more were preparing to raise breaching ladders and behind them, hundreds waited to climb to the top of the wall.

Xith regarded Seth, the elf's prowess in battle was awe-inspiring. In the midst of the enemy ranks, Seth had leapt from his horse, seemingly undaunted by the fact that he had been surrounded. Now, all around him lay the dead and the dying.

"I wish I had a hundred like him," shouted Captain Mikhal to Xith above the din of the battle.

"I wish there were a hundred like him." Xith pointed to the breached section of the wall. "Do you think we can reach it?"

Captain Mikhal's eyes went wide, apparently he hadn't seen the breach until now. He raised his sword high, and behind him a trumpeter's call rang out. He pointed his sword in the direction of the wall.

"To the wall," he shouted and charged.

The trumpeter's call rang out again, and while the bulk of the Kingdom forces were caught in attacks, hundreds rallied and raced after their commander.

Xith turned his mount about and charged in Seth's direction. Two bolts of lightning, cast first from his left hand then his right, cleared the way through the enemy ranks. He wheeled his mount in front of Seth. "Now is not your time to journey to Great-Father, Brother Seth, they have need of your skills upon the walls. Climb on!"

Xith helped Seth onto his mount.

"Hold on tight," Xith said. He kicked his mount sharply.

They raced off.

***

Galan had followed Seth in his thoughts, looking out through his eyes to the battlefield. She had watched the green and gold of the Kingdom banners clash with the blue and black. For a time, it seemed those of the green and gold held a strategic advantage on the field, where the others held an advantage solely in numbers.

Then she had lost contact with Seth's mind. She knew only that he was caught up in the frenzy of battle and she had been content to look down from her vantage point to the city below. The boy, Vilmos, walked silently at her side. She could sense conflicting emotions in him and a great urge to race to the field to join his master.

When they were directly north of the city, Galan and Vilmos began the long westward circle. Here they followed the rim of the valley. The sounds of the battle were reduced to a faint din in the distance and both the attackers and defenders were reduced to tiny figures moving about on the fields around the city's walls.

Galan lashed out with her thoughts, *Where are you, Seth?*

Galan felt Vilmos' subconscious shiver at the sound of the voice in his mind. *I am sorry, I should have directed the thoughts. I am ill accustomed to your ways, please forgive me.*

❧ The Kingdoms & The Elves ❧

Vilmos asked, "Can you really talk across such a distance?"

Only if Brother Seth maintains the link and as long as we do not journey too much farther away from the—

Galan broke off as Seth's vision filled her mind's eye with second sight. Seth was atop the east wall. The wind was blowing in his hair, and he was looking across the basin to the battlefield. Still, the green and gold were holding their own. With the Kingdom defenders back in control of the east and south walls, they could now lend considerable aid to the Kingdom soldiers in the field. Catapults hurled rocks. Arrows from Kingdom archers rained down upon the enemy. But the enemy still held a tremendous advantage in sheer numbers. They outnumbered the Kingdom soldiers at least five to one.

Several large columns of the enemy army had fallen back to regroup. Three lines of shield bearers hundreds long amassed. Behind them, bowmen, prepared to fire on the move, would provide cover, while swordsmen and pikemen waited to strike. The enemy commanders rallied them, then ordered the attack. The shield bearers, pikemen and swordsmen surged forward, a great moving wall that clashed with the first line of the Kingdom defense.

Enemy bowmen focused on the heart of Kingdom defenses. Pikemen used the shield bearers for cover, their long-pole arms felling nearly all who came against them. Swordsmen filled in the gaps of those who fell, and again and again the enemy wall surged forward. In short order, they cut off several groups of Kingdom soldiers from the main forces and gained control of the field.

Vilmos grabbed Galan's hand. "Look. They march, from the

east!"

Seth, to the west, the forces west of the city are on the march. They aim to come up from the south. You must find a way to bolster—

***

—the forces upon the southern wall. I will pray for you and for reinforcements, sent Galan.

Seth severed the link and turned his attention to the defenders on the wall. One of them must be in command. He watched for a moment to see who was giving the orders, but there was so much chaos it was difficult to tell. He stopped a man rushing past.

Who leads?

A puzzled frown crossed the man's face. He turned and pointed, then hurried off. Seth raced off in the opposite direction.

Do you lead? Seth asked.

"I am Sergeant Danyel'."

This man was also puzzled but was too exhausted to understand why. Seth switched to spoken words. "From the west, the enemy comes. You must send reinforcements to the southern wall."

"There are no reinforcements. This is it. The Father must truly hate us."

"The enemy does not attack from the north. How many men do you have positioned there?"

Sergeant Danyel' wiped blood and grime from his brow. "Twenty. No, fifteen."

"And you will have to bring more from the west and the east."

"I cannot bring any from the east, and in the west I have more wounded than able." Sergeant Danyel' stopped abruptly, cocked his head, then reached for his sword. "Who are you? You wear Kingdom insignia, yet—"

There is not time to explain who I am, you must trust me, you simply must. I rode in from the east with Captain Mikhal, it was he who gave me this. Seth indicated the green and gold cloth tied around his right arm.

Sergeant Danyel' furrowed his brows momentarily, then grabbed one of the soldiers rushing by. "Send runners. Strip the north wall, any able-bodied men from the west wall and twenty from the east to the south wall."

"Sir, I go to the north wall. You know the enemy hasn't attacked at all from the north, Chancellor Van'te expects a strike there next."

"That was an order! I will deal with Chancellor Van'te if need be." Sergeant Danyel' stumbled, and Seth had to support him or else he would have collapsed.

The soldier held his ground, eyeing his sergeant and Seth.

Lead me to this Chancellor Van'te and I will talk to him, Seth told the soldier, then turning back to Danyel', he said, *You must rest, you are of little use in this condition.*

"No, I will go with you. Soldier, lead the way!"

***

Arrows poured down upon them like a ceaseless rain. Xith extended the radius of his magic shield to protect those around him, but could only extend its protective envelope so far. He was tired and his mind was on other things, mainly trying to pinpoint a weakness in the enemy lines through which they could escape back to the Kingdom lines.

While they had managed to push the attackers back from the walls, the enemy had only to regroup and come again. In the end, it had cost the Kingdom forces dearly. Of the hundreds of men that had rallied and raced after their commander to the base of the wall, fewer than one hundred remained. Most were foot soldiers, a scattered few were horse soldiers. Yet, while they were cut off from their lines and trapped in a sea of the enemy, they did not relent. They were determined to keep the enemy at bay.

Xith sat his mount beside Father Jacob and Captain Mikhal. The Kingdom commander was nearly exhausted, but remained tall in his saddle. There was defiant pride in his eyes. His soldiers guarded him with a fierceness rarely seen, and with their lives.

Xith wheeled his mount in a tight circle, continuing his search for a weakness in the enemy lines. He knew Captain Mikhal must survive, for in him lay the power to deliver the city from the hands of the enemy. The Kingdom forces were rapidly losing momentum. Without the leadership of their commander, and more importantly the strength he lent to his men, all would soon be forever lost. The time to act was now.

Xith's mount whinnied and reared. Xith fought to control it, and as he struggled with the animal, a flash of color waving not far off caught his eye. He steadied the horse. He stared, squinted, his eyes went wide as he realized what he saw was a royal banner. For an instant, as the press of bodies around the King parted, Xith looked straight at King Jarom.

Xith wasn't the only one to see the banner. When Xith looked back to Captain Mikhal, he found that the captain had already raised his sword. Xith knew at once the captain was preparing for a direct charge against the monarch's defenses, a charge Xith had to stop before it was too late.

But when their commander raised his blade high, the ten remaining horse soldiers around him did likewise. Before Xith could act, Captain Mikhal dropped his sword and spurred his mount. His men followed. The foot soldiers parted to let the riders through, then took up position along the riders' flanks.

Xith held his ground for a moment, considering what to do. Again, he saw Vostok's royal banner fluttering in the wind, so close, yet so far. It was a hopeless charge, Xith knew it, but he also knew he could not stop it. He followed.

Abruptly the call of countless trumpets broke the air. Fighting on both sides broke off. Captain Mikhal and his men cut short their charge. All eyes turned southward. Poised along a ridge of the foothills was a line of horse soldiers a thousand across. The Kingdom forces began to whoop and cheer. Prince Valam and reinforcements had surely arrived.

A second time, trumpet calls broke the air. The riders began their charge, a great black wave racing downward. The Kingdomers continued to whoop and cheer, then gradually their cries turned to murmurs of dismay, for behind this massive wave came a line of flag bearers. The banners they bore were bold red and stark white, and not Kingdom green and gold. Behind the flag bearers came long lines of foot soldiers. It was not Prince Valam at all, but the army of the Kingdom of Sever.

***

Vilmos' mouth fell open. He gawked at the red and white banners, and the force of thousands on the move to the battle around

Quashan'. The Kingdom soldiers would soon be completely overwhelmed, and if there had been even the smallest of hopes for winning the battle before, it died with the arrival of the main host from Sever's forces.

Before he knew what he was doing, Vilmos found he was racing down the hillside.

Vilmos, stop, called out Galan, *you will only get yourself killed. We are to wait here and give instructions when reinforcements arrive.*

Vilmos paused only to turn back and regard Galan. Magic flowed through him like a tidal wave. His eyes focused with rage told her what he couldn't say. Then he cast off the voice in his mind that told him what he didn't want to hear and raced off.

Worriedly, he studied the distant battlefield. King Jarom's forces had fallen back to re-form and wait for the fresh troops. The Kingdom soldiers also regrouped, but they did not wait to attack afterward.

Vilmos, panting and straining for breath, forced himself to maintain a breakneck pace. Behind him, Galan with her longer strides was catching up to him. Vilmos fought to stay ahead of her but couldn't, and soon they were running side by side.

Vilmos, what good will dying do? This is pointless.

"I am a magic-user, just as Xith. I do what I must."

You are an apprentice.

Vilmos didn't answer, he pushed himself to race still faster. Sever's horsemen had already clashed with what remained of Quashan's garrison. The Kingdom soldiers fell back, tried frantically to re-form, but each time they formed a hasty shield wall it crumbled, forcing another retreat. Soon it became painfully clear that the Kingdom army was on the run.

Only a hundred yards to go now and Vilmos would be on the flat fields surrounding Quashan'. There he could stretch out his legs, and there he was sure he would leave Galan behind. He ran to the pace of the thump-thump in his ears, which drowned out the cries of despair and anguish that the wind carried. Once on the flat fields, Vilmos stretched out his legs, lengthening his strides. As he did this, his foot caught Galan's. Both stumbled and fell.

Vilmos was quick to regain his feet. He screamed at Galan, "You did that on purpose!"

Galan turned Vilmos about, so he was staring up at the valley's rim from the direction they had just come from. He had just started to protest when he saw them, a line of horse soldiers. The banners at the fore were green and gold. Prince Valam had come. He had found Keeper Martin and those of Imtal garrison.

Behind the horse soldiers came the foot soldiers, thousands of them, and far more than Vilmos or Galan had anticipated. Amidst the green and gold banners were banners bearing a blue circle on a field of white. Galan asked Vilmos without words and strangely with only emotions who the others were. Vilmos could only shrug. He didn't know.

Prince Valam, there! shouted Galan.

"Where?"

There! repeated Galan. She grabbed Vilmos' hand and pulled him to a start, and he chased after her.

Chapter Thirteen:
Last Play

It was now late afternoon. During the day the battle had taken many turns. The arrival of nearly ten thousand troops, Imtal soldiers and free men, had changed the tide of the battle for a time. Still, this had only made the field more even and not equal.

Adrina was in the middle of relating the story of their journey and of how Keeper Martin and Captain Adylton had managed to persuade the free men of Mir and Veter to join the Kingdom's cause. "Most are oarsmen from the free city fleet, not soldiers, though still good with a blade," Adrina said. "Gold surely persuaded their loyalty, also a fear of losing their freedom, for after he had captured the whole of the South, King Jarom surely wouldn't have let the Free Cities remain outside his rule."

"Surely we cannot just sit here," Vilmos said. "We must do something."

"I aim to do something, all right." Adrina grinned. "Tell me exactly what the lady told each of you. She did speak to each of you, right?"

Galan and Vilmos quickly told Adrina what they remembered of the conversation, though much of it seemed a blur.

"She spoke of choices being like the branches of trees and for right or wrong you follow one or the other, and of good and evil," concluded Vilmos.

Adrina asked, "Did she tell you to remember something?"

Vilmos was pacing. Adrina knew he was growing restless. She turned to Galan, and found an unexpected expression in the elf's eyes. "What is it Galan, what do you see?"

Galan was staring off into the distance, her eyes were unfocussed. *Seth upon the walls.*

"Really, you can see him from here?" asked Adrina.

Galan didn't answer. She was apparently lost in what she was seeing and Vilmos explained what little he knew of her gift, which he deemed akin to corporeal stasis.

It is not, Galan said, *it is a projecting of thoughts. I can project feelings and images too.*

"Like an image in a dream," Adrina said.

Galan didn't reply—she was again distracted by what she saw.

"Is there a way we can see as well?" Adrina asked.

Perhaps.

Suddenly, Adrina saw Seth standing atop the upper battlements along Quashan's southern wall. She could feel the wind blowing through his hair and the despair ravaging his heart. Seth's emotions flowed to Adrina, mixing with her own, and soon despair ravaged her heart as well. The enemy had breached the southern gates of the city and a wave of humanity was pouring in. Torches were being distributed and many buildings were already burning. Cries of panic rose; she heard women and children crying as they ran from the homes they fled.

When Galan broke the link, Adrina found she was trembling beyond her control and her cheeks were wet with tears. From their vantage point, they saw the billows of smoke, and eventually the flames as well.

Adrina asked, "Is there no hope?"

Neither Vilmos nor Galan spoke.

Adrina turned to the group of guardsmen who Valam had insisted remain to see to her protection in case the worst happened. Their faces were racked with anguish and lament. She knew they wanted to join the fight, though it would surely cost them their lives.

She stood and wiped the tears from her eyes.

"I order you into battle!" Adrina shouted.

The ranking soldier said, "His Highness ordered us to remain."

Adrina glared. "And I am ordering you into battle! Now, mount your horses and go."

"We cannot."

"If Quashan' falls, I will have no need for fifty guards. I will have no need for guards at all." Adrina turned away from the speaker. "I will count to five, when I turn around you *will* be gone, and I will speak never a word about this. One, two—"

Adrina waited until the sound of hooves mixed in with the din of the battle before she turned back around. She was surprised to find that six guardsmen remained.

She glared at them, but they held their ground.

"We must stay," one of the men said. "If it comes to it, we will ensure you reach Imtal."

Adrina didn't offer a response.

Vilmos seemed suddenly inspired by the sight of the retreating guardsmen and there was the same twinkle in his eye that Adrina had seen in her brother's eyes earlier. "Take my hand," Vilmos told Galan.

Vilmos' eyes glossed over, and it seemed he was in a trance. Adrina and Galan waited. Adrina was unsure what to expect.

After a time, Vilmos released Galan's hand. "In the foothills, the Wolmerrelle. Erravane." His voice betrayed dismay. "William of Sever, she certainly is seeking him out."

Galan's voice whispered in Adrina's mind, *You will find help in a most unlikely source.*

"To think, I once called him cousin," Adrina said, "If only we understood why he turned against Great Kingdom."

"Perhaps we do," said a voice from behind them.

The Kingdom soldiers rushed to protect Adrina. Adrina, Vilmos and Galan turned around and stared into the afternoon shadows. A man with gray hair and a distinctive salt-and-pepper colored beard slowly made his way from the shadows. Adrina said, "Keeper Martin."

Recognizing the lore keeper, the soldiers backed down.

"You must excuse me," Keeper Martin said, "I have been listening to your conversation for some time. I circled back about an hour ago."

Keeper Martin walked toward them. Adrina saw that his face was drawn and pale, and then she saw the deep stain of blood on the right side of his cloak.

"An arrow." Keeper Martin said simply as he eased to a sitting position.

Adrina's eyes went wide.

"Yes, I will live." Martin motioned for them to sit. Adrina, Galan and Vilmos sat.

"I was in Gregortonn when King Charles was poisoned and, finally, I understand why King William has joined with King Jarom."

"King? What—" Adrina began.

Jacob raised a silencing hand. "King Charles has passed on. The grippe took Phillip. William is heir. As you can see by the display in the field, there was no contest to his ascension. Yet, I am sure that it is with little pride and no love that the army of Sever sides with Vostok.

"The truth is that I myself did not understand what I had seen in Gregortonn until some hours ago, but by then I thought it too late to act on what I knew. Yet, I can see the error of that now and you are responsible for opening my eyes."

Adrina furrowed her eyebrows.

"Babbling, aren't I? Perhaps—" Keeper Martin coughed and gripped his side. "—it is the wound. Yet, I tend to do that normally. It is the green and the gold."

"Green and gold?" Adrina asked.

"All along I was sure agents of King Jarom had somehow seized power in Sever's capital, for you see, I saw through the disguises and when I saw banners of green and gold—Kingdom colors—to me such colors were not out of place, but those of

Sever knew at once the colors were foreign."

Keeper Martin's face became extremely pale. He bit back pain, then took a long drink from a wine-bag. "Do you understand?"

"I am beginning to," Adrina said.

"Brother Galan, as Lore Keeper of Great Kingdom, I know much more about your kind than the average Kingdomer, still your gifts are truly amazing. Can you truly project images into the minds of others?"

May I? asked Galan, suggesting she wanted to take a closer look at Martin's side. Keeper Martin nodded approval and then seemed not to notice Galan's hands probing the outside of the wound. *You did not remove the shaft of the arrow.*

"The shaft snapped."

Shock crossed Adrina's face as Galan's hand melted into Martin's side. Keeper Martin gave no indication of sudden pain, in fact, he seemed at ease. Adrina, torn between repulsion and attraction, watched. The skin around Galan's wrist rippled as if fluid, and as if nothing was happening, Keeper Martin turned to Vilmos and said, "What little I know of the Watcher, through Father Jacob, leads me to believe that you are gifted with the forbidden as is he, and while I do not condone its use, I believe, as does Father Jacob, exceptions must be allowed if they are for a greater good. Yet, you are also from Sever. Yes?"

"My home is Tabborrath Village," Vilmos said.

Martin said, "Your Highness, come here, let me look at you."

Adrina didn't move. Galan was withdrawing her hand and in it, she held the broken arrow.

"Your Highness," Martin repeated.

Adrina looked up. Martin looked into her eyes. "You are the image of your mother, and Queen Elthia as well. Can you braid your hair in a triple braid and let it flow over your right shoulder?"

Adrina caught a glimpse of a pink-yellow glow out of the corner of her eye. She looked back to Martin's wound to find it was gone, as if it had vanished. Adrina turned back to Martin and said, "I think you should rest, you are not thinking clearly."

"On the contrary, I have never thought more clearly." Keeper Martin waved one of the guardsmen over. He was a short, thin fellow. "Soldier, change clothes with the lad here, he will have need of your uniform."

***

Xith kneeled beside Captain Mikhal and cradled the man's head in his hands. Most of the southern quarter of Quashan' was ablaze, and a full evacuation had begun. The Kingdom army was divided and they were now defending against two fronts. King Jarom's foot soldiers came from the west. The army of Sever pressed from the east. The horse soldiers of both kingdoms controlled the middle of the field.

It all seemed so utterly hopeless.

"Can you save him?" Xith asked Father Jacob who also kneeled beside the fallen commander.

"The wound is grievous, I can only ease his suffering."

"Do so, he has earned a peaceful passing from this life."

Xith had been sore pressed to convince Captain Mikhal that his men needed his continued strength and guidance and that a single last rallying of his horse soldiers for a final charge would have been sheer folly. Xith found it a bittersweet irony that the commander had met the lethal blow while trying to return to the ranks of his soldiers a second time.

"He is gone," whispered Jacob.

"He was a brave man."

Father Jacob bent his head for a moment of prayer and Xith did likewise.

Shouts erupted from not far off. "Fall back, fall back," the voices screamed.

The former sub-commander beside them stood and urged them to retreat. Xith and Jacob stood and followed the new commander as his forces fell back to regroup.

***

Beside Adrina, Galan and Vilmos marched silently. Adrina could only vaguely see the silhouettes of the five soldiers who preceded them amidst the glare of the setting sun. Slowly though, more and more shadows shrouded the foothills and nightfall steadily approached.

Vilmos, dressed in the guardsman's uniform, held tightly the prize Keeper Martin had given him. He was their eyes. He kept watch from overhead and Galan at his side directed him. She read his thoughts, and thus they were able to steer clear of any patrols set up in anticipation of an ambush as the field became blurred.

Keeper Martin's plan had seemed bold as he had revealed it to them, but now as they moved ever closer to the ranks of Sever's army, it also seemed suddenly desperate and simple. They were to sneak into William's camp, find his tent and convince him that Great Kingdom had no part in his father's death.

The guardsmen disguised as Sever soldiers and the banner

Vilmos held but did not display would help them on their way. Still, the most difficult part—moving through the camp, finding William and convincing him—would fall to Adrina, Vilmos and Galan alone, and mostly to Adrina. She wasn't entirely sure she could convince William of anything, though she knew she must try.

***

Darkness fell, and still the battle for Quashan' raged.

Prince Valam conferred with his field commanders, the captains of the Imtal and Quashan' garrisons. Only a short time ago his forces had finally managed to break through the enemy lines to join with the soldiers of Quashan', and he had just now learned of the death of Quashan's commander.

Kingdom forces held the base of the southern and eastern walls of the city, yet the fire within the city still burned out of control. The enemy came at them along two fronts, but fortunately could no longer attack from the rear or squeeze them into a killing zone. At last, they had driven back the enemy horse soldiers and erected an inner and outer defensive line. In an ironic twist, they had taken control of the trenches dug by those that had besieged the city initially, and it was this that was helping them fend off the superior force.

"The attack slows, Your Highness," Captain Adylton said. He wiped fresh blood from his face and sheathed his blade. "I answered the call as soon as I could."

A soldier offered the captain water and he drank heavily. Captain Adylton continued, "It looks as if they'll soon fall back to their lines. The night comes."

Prince Valam said, "That is indeed news worth waiting for."

Valam surveyed his commanders. "Has anyone seen Captain Berre?"

A sergeant with a soot-covered face answered. "He commands on the left flank, Your Highness. He sent me in his stead. He has the devil's own fury in his eyes. His home, a wife and three children, were along Cooper's Walk."

"Stand at ease sergeant." Valam looked to the burning city, then to Captain Adylton. "What of the other Imtal commanders?"

"Captain Ghenson's position was overrun. He was dragged from his mount, I believe he is dead."

Valam turned to the sergeant. "What news from the left flank?"

"Your Highness—"

"Save the pleasantries for another place and time. Be frank and quick."

"The line holds, the men are tired, hungry and thirsty. The wounded and the dying lie about the field. Their sappers are digging another trench line, and Captain Berre fears it is a sign they await reinforcements."

Valam gripped the sergeant's shoulder, then turned to Father Jacob. "Father Jacob?" he said.

Father Jacob stood a little taller and nodded.

"At last, we have a stable position. Care of the wounded is in your hands. I want all wounded who can still walk, but cannot wield a sword, on relief brigade. Without food and water, soldiers cannot fight."

The soot-faced sergeant's downtrodden expression brightened.

Xith stepped forward. "May I speak?"

"Speak freely."

"Light skirmishes and raids will continue through the night, the enemy hopes to keep us expecting an attack that will not come and to wear us out. An all out attack will not come until just before dawn, but if we switch to a defensive and do not continue to press the attack, all will surely be lost come morning."

Valam was puzzled. "How can you possibly know this?"

Father Jacob said, "There are those who have divine gifts of sight, and Master Xith is one of them. You trusted him before, you must trust him again. Without him Quashan' would have already fallen, and none of us would be standing here now."

Valam extended his hand to Xith's shoulder. "I am sorry, it has been a trying day. You must know that you have my eternal gratitude and when this is all over, one way or another, I will repay you."

"If you want to repay me, do what I say." Xith paused, and for a moment, it seemed as if he heard something far off. Valam heard it too, perhaps it was the call of an eagle from high overhead, but he couldn't be sure. "Before moonrise, every available man must be mustered and assembled for an all out assault against Sever's army. At precisely moonrise, the attack must begin."

"We cannot desert the left flank," interrupted the sergeant. "There are two enemy armies—"

Valam raised a silencing hand and Xith continued. "Yes, it is very important that the enemy not know we have stripped our left flank. Moonrise is not for some hours and the night sky looks to be dark and clouded. We can use this to our advantage…"

***

Vilmos unfurled Sever's banner. Adrina tried to imagine that she heard it flapping in the wind instead of pitiful moans and screams of agony. She forced herself to maintain a steady pace. Her heart pounded in her ears and she bit her cheek to remind herself to stay calm. Frantic thoughts flashed through her mind and more than once she almost cried out at the ghastly sight of the dead and the dying that littered William's camp from end to end.

For a moment, Adrina thought of Emel and wondered where he was amidst the fighting, then the thought was gone. Ahead lay a tent with many guards posted around it. Adrina was sure it was William's. Expectantly, she inhaled a breath and held it, but when Galan continued past the tent without even turning an eye toward it, Adrina let the breath slip out.

"You passed his tent, is something wrong?" Adrina whispered.

There is nothing wrong, said Galan, carefully directing the thoughts.

After passing the last tent on the end, Galan paused. *This is William's tent. The other was meant to catch the eye of anyone bold enough to sneak into the camp.*

Galan did not hesitate long, instead she continued until she found a place with few campfires and no torches. *There were two guards just inside the entrance, but cleanly out of view. William sits at a table with his back to the guards. There was another in the tent, but he was preparing to leave.*

Vilmos tossed aside the banner. "You read their thoughts?"

In a way, yes.

Adrina asked, "Is there a chance we can replace the guards with our own?"

One of the guardsmen stepped forward. "We will try. They are surely hungry or tired, or both. I can tell you there have been many times I wished for relief and would never have questioned it if it came."

Galan smiled, seemingly approving the show of bravery. She closed her eyes for a moment. *They are both hungry and tired. You are quite wise.*

"I am but a simple soldier who knows what it is to stand watch." The soldier broke off, his face showing concern.

"Go quickly," Adrina said, "may Great-Father watch over you."

Two soldiers slipped away.

While they waited, Adrina took in the activity around them. Everywhere soldiers hurried about the camp, singly, in pairs, and in large groups. The camp was in a state of confused frenzy, but this was changing, order was being restored from chaos. The sound of the battle was fading. More and more fires were raised both along the camp's perimeter and its interior, and lines of torches were being put in place to mark hastily cleared paths.

Princess Adrina?

"What is it, Galan?" Adrina whispered.

They are inside.

Adrina saw two figures leave the tent. "Is it safe to proceed?"

Galan said, *It would seem so.*

Quietly the small group moved toward the tent.

"What would you have us do, Your Highness?" asked one of the three remaining guardsmen.

"When we reach the tent, we will go in, you three will continue past. Do not stray far though, we may have need of your sword arms. Keep a close eye on the tent, and do not start a fight unless it is absolutely necessary. If an alarm is sounded, we will surely never leave this camp."

At the front of the tent, they stopped. Adrina signaled to the guardsmen to continue on their way. They did so reluctantly.

Adrina started toward the tent's entrance. Suddenly everything Keeper Martin had told Adrina flooded through her mind. She knew that in order to convince William of the truth, she must first find confidence in herself. Still, she didn't see how her resemblance to Queen Elthia would help anything. Or why it was important that Vilmos was a native Severian. Nor did she really understand how Galan was supposed to project Keeper Martin's memories of Gregortonn into William's mind when Keeper Martin wasn't even with them.

Galan grabbed Adrina's arm and pulled her back. *Wait, there is something wrong. I am not sure—No, I am sure, Erravane.*

"The Wolmerrelle," Vilmos said. He gasped. "We must act now or all this will be for nothing."

Galan stopped Vilmos from hastily running into the tent and indicated that they should move back in the direction they had just come from. *As unlikely as it seems Erravane's presence may actually help us. We should wait to see what occurs.*

"I agree," Adrina said, "we should—" From far off the sound of angry voices exploded into the air, followed by panic-filled screams. More shouting followed. Soon an alarm was sweeping through the camp.

Frenzy followed. The camp was in an uproar. Men were running about the camp screaming, "To battle! To battle! The enemy comes!" Then, Adrina heard shouting and screams from

William's tent. She turned bewildered eyes to Vilmos and Galan. Together they rushed into William's tent.

The two guards lay face down in the dirt. Adrina did not doubt that they were dead. Apparently Erravane had cut her way in through the back of the tent and aimed to go out the same way. In a half-human half-animal state, Erravane was dragging William out of the tent. Abruptly she changed directions and pushed her way back into the tent. Behind her came the three Kingdom guardsmen, their swords drawn.

Erravane spun around. Her eyes were wild. "Princess Adrina, you of all people should not stand in my way. William's disappearance will most certainly serve you."

William shouted, "She aims to kill me."

"Hush, or I'll rip out your tongue, I will only kill you at the end and though you deserve much anguish for abandoning me, I will do it swiftly."

"Even William doesn't deserve to die," Adrina said, her voice strong and with no hint of the alarm that raged through her mind. "Release him, or you will never escape from this camp."

"If I do not escape, neither will you."

Vilmos pushed past Adrina. Blue-white fire danced around his hands. "Xith warned you not to meddle in affairs that do not concern you."

"It is you, the boy who killed—" Erravane was shocked. "No, it cannot be. You and the Watcher should be—"

"Not in the Vangar, we are here—" As Vilmos spoke, he walked slowly toward Erravane, his hands poised menacingly "— And, should he find you, he will most assuredly keep his promise."

Erravane howled and with inhuman strength hurled William at Vilmos. She turned to make an escape, the guards barred her way. Adrina knew for certain they'd be killed if they tried to stop her.

"No!" Adrina screamed. "Let her pass."

The guards stepped aside and Erravane fled into the night.

Vilmos and William were in a jumble on the ground. Galan and Adrina helped them to their feet. William's eyes were agape and shock was evident on his face. He started to say something, but before he could say anything, a soldier rushed into tent. Adrina turned about. The Kingdom guardsmen began shouting and rushed forward to intercept the soldier who had drawn his sword and also had begun shouting.

The Kingdom guardsmen engaged the lone soldier of Sever.

Adrina began shouting, "No, no, Stop," but the combatants didn't.

The soldier lay dead on the dirt floor before other soldiers answering his call rushed into the tent. Soon the three Kingdom guardsmen were being pushed back by the sheer number of newcomers arrived to save their king.

Adrina turned to William. "Do something, make them stop!"

William seemed disoriented.

"Do something," Adrina repeated. She grabbed William about the shoulders and shook him.

"I am in no danger, I think, I mean—I need to sort this out." William paused, flustered. "Sergeant, soldiers, I order you to halt!"

The soldiers grudgingly broke off the attack. William pointed to two of them. "Find Commander Stenocco, tell him to come at once. Five more stand guard, the rest of you outside."

The soldiers didn't move.

"Throw down your weapons," Adrina told the Kingdom guardsmen. They hesitated. "Do it!"

Their swords clanked as they hit the ground.

A puzzled frown returned to William's face as he turned to Adrina. "Why did you save me? I mean, Erravane was right, you should have rejoiced. Why are you in my camp in the first place, if it is not to kill me?"

"We came to talk." Adrina wanted to say more but she was trembling and there were tears in her eyes. Suddenly it seemed lead weights were around her shoulders and her legs wanted to collapse under the weight. "May I sit?"

"A chair," William said.

A soldier quickly brought a chair.

Adrina cleared her throat, then looked to Vilmos and Galan in turn. She started speaking, determined to convince William using Keeper Martin's plan. Yet somehow, things didn't come out the way she planned, and instead she told him everything the plan entailed. She explained how they had come to the camp and sneaked through it intent on finding him, how they had planned to trick him and finally how they had planned to convince him of the truth. During the telling Sever's commander hurried into the tent but William ordered silence.

Adrina concluded by saying, "I tell you the truth when I say I harbor no hate in my heart for all you have done. I know what it is to grieve for one so dear it seems they are all you had in the world. I know what it is like to feel you are all alone. I know how such loss can cloud your mind and make you want to lash out at all the world, but if you loved your father, and I know you truly did, you will listen to reason. Great Kingdom had no part in your father's death. This you must believe."

Indignation crossed William's face. "How can you possibly know what I feel? How can you possibly know what it is like to lose a mother, father, and brother all in the space of a few years?" William's eyes turn wild. His tone became icy cold. "Kill them, kill them all!"

The Kingdom guardsmen raced for their swords. Adrina leapt from her chair and started screaming at William. Galan grabbed Adrina and pushed her back. Vilmos stepped in front of them both.

There was joy in Commander Stenocco's eyes as he withdrew his great sword from its sheath. He ordered his men to stand at ease. "Leave them to me," he said arrogantly, "I want them all."

The Kingdom guardsmen held their ground as the enemy commander advanced on them. When he was within striking distance, Commander Stenocco stopped and laughed, mocking the tension on the guardsmen's faces. He spat, then with surprising speed, heaved his massive blade toward them. Adrina squeezed her eyes together and winced in anticipation of the sound of clashing blades. When she heard a dull thud instead, she opened her eyes, expecting the worst. The worst hadn't happened, however. Nothing had happened.

Commander Stenocco's eyes were wide and filled with rage. He lashed out with his sword. Yet the sword couldn't reach its mark. Again and again Adrina heard a dull thud. For a moment, the commander stood unmoving, a muscle in his cheek twitched nervously, then he cast aside his sword and began ramming the unseen barrier.

Adrina was as confused as the enemy commander was, she turned to Galan. Galan pointed to Vilmos.

"Princess," Vilmos said, "I cannot hold him back long. Do what you must!"

Adrina's thoughts spun inward. She turned back to William and felt suddenly sick to her stomach. She knew what she had to do—something she wished someone had done to her long ago. She struck William across the face with the back of her hand. "How dare you speak to me like that!" she screamed at him, then with her eyes she backed him into his chair.

"King Charles is gone, your self-pity will not bring him back! Great Kingdom and Sever have always been the strongest of allies. My father, King Andrew, has no desire to sit upon Sever's throne. That seat belongs to the line of Charles, to you... Think. Who stands to gain the most from such treachery? Think, and no longer let blind rage control your actions."

For a long time, William said nothing, then he turned to the soldiers inside the tent and dismissed them all save for his commander. "It is no easy thing to stop what has already begun," William finally told Adrina, "I know you are sincere and though I want to believe you, I cannot. You spoke of proof. If you have proof that King Jarom was behind the poisoning of my father, I would hear it."

Commander Stenocco screamed, "This is a trick, their forces attack as we speak!"

William raised his hand, commanding silence. "You spoke of

proof, I would hear it," he repeated.

Adrina turned to Galan. "Are you ready?"

***

False dawn was on the horizon and still the battle raged. Seth looked down from atop the wall to the fields south of the city. The Kingdom forces were falling back to re-form for another charge, to the west Sever's army was also regrouping and to the east King Jarom's army was mustering for their first attack of the new day. Vostok's soldiers were fresh, few soldiers stood between them and the middle of Prince Valam's camp as the bulk of the Kingdom army was engaged in the fighting to the west. Seth knew that once the attack came the camp would be overrun.

Seth watched the men upon the walls prepare for the attack. Bowmen notched arrows. Soldiers loaded catapults. Others hunkered down behind the battlements and waited to counter the press of enemy siege ladders.

Trumpets chanted to the east. Vostok's army began to form in long lines. Shield bearers at the fore followed by pikemen, swordsmen and lastly archers. Horse soldiers in column formation waited with swords raised high.

The trumpets sounded again. Thousands of foot soldiers screamed and charged. Seth turned his eyes westward, expecting Sever's army to begin their charge. They had re-formed, but held their ground. Poised to strike to the west, the Kingdom army also waited. Their rear ranks began to turn about and prepare a defensive, but did not move fearing a deception.

Perplexed, Seth watched the two unmoving armies. He wavered his gaze, trying to see why neither attacked. *Was there something on the field between them?*

Galan? Seth called out.

Seth, came Galan's voice into his mind

What is happening?

Sever's army is quitting the field, Galan replied, and it was then that Seth saw the white flag and six figures moving toward the Kingdom lines.

Seth was puzzled. *But to the east, the attack comes.*

By the Mother, I did not realize—you must find Prince Valam. William has decided to quit the field. Seth, he knows the truth. But he also says he cannot fight against King Jarom.

Vostok's army came. The clash began. The Kingdom army seemed unsure of which direction to defend against. Seth started running along the top of the wall. He was sure disaster waited in this indecision. He tried reaching the prince's mind, but he had no idea where Prince Valam was among the mass of men in the frenzied camp below.

Sergeant Danyel'? Chancellor Van'te? Seth screamed.

Fatigue clouded Seth's mind, allowing panic and dread to flood over him. He raced faster and faster. Then Sever's army began to quit the field, and when it was clear they were not just falling back and were actually retiring, a wave of cheers erupted from the mouths of the Kingdom soldiers. The men atop the walls also began to cheer.

Seth stopped running. The whole of the Kingdom army turned about, and weary or not, they began a driving charge. King Jarom's army hadn't anticipated such a massive counterstrike. Their shield wall was weak and it fell quickly.

✿❀ The Kingdoms & The Elves ✿❀

In retaliation, Vostok's horse soldiers began their assault, but this came too late. The two armies were too intertwined and the enemy riders trampled their own soldiers as well as Kingdom soldiers. And when the riders met the first solid Kingdom line, horses and men collided, lances met readied swords and pikes, and large numbers of riders were pulled from their mounts or had mounts cut out from beneath them.

The Kingdom army had its own horse soldiers and they were driving into the heart of the enemy army. Vostok's army, stunned and surprised, could only fall back again and again, but without support from the other flank they no longer had superior numbers in the field. It was now they who were outnumbered.

One last time the army of Vostok tried to raise a defense so they could re-form, but this was shattered quickly and the Kingdom army made good their rout. The men upon the walls began cheering louder and louder. For days their city had been besieged and now the enemy was on the run. They were elated and suddenly no longer weary.

Seth watched the Kingdom horse soldiers pursue the enemy army to the valley's rim and beyond. It was there that Seth lost sight of them. He too was joyous, and he joined in their cheers.

***

A full celebration was underway.

The fires in the city were at last extinguished and rebuilding would begin as soon as possible. Already priests and priestesses had arrived, answering Prince Valam's call for aid. The Priestesses of the Mother were caring for the hundreds wounded. The Priests of the Father were interring the dead upon the fields south of

Quashan', and the former battlefields would forever more stand as grim reminders of the devastation wrought by even the briefest of wars. Great Kingdom's losses had been heavy .

Adrina's joy was tainted with sorrow. She felt so alone, even though Galan was beside her. Vilmos had gone off in search of Xith, and while Adrina was sure Galan would have rather sought out Seth, Galan had stayed with Adrina to comfort her. Emel had not been among the fit or the wounded, and she had searched through every one of the dozens of relief houses set up to care for the wounded. The only thing she could do now was to search among the dead for his body, a task that seemed too grim for her to bear alone, yet she was determined to find Emel and to say her goodbyes.

"Father Jacob," Adrina called out.

A very weary Father Jacob turned to greet her. He took her hand. "Your Highness, I have heard of your deed, you have done well, very well indeed." Jacob grinned, and a bit of fatigue lifted from his eyes. "I knew you would."

"Emel," Adrina said, "you haven't..."

"No, I have not seen Emel, yet I do not think you will find him here."

"I have looked everywhere but here, Father Jacob." Adrina was in tears. "He is nowhere to be found."

"I have lain to rest too many familiar faces, I remember each, and none was Emel's. Perhaps you searched the wrong places."

Adrina was convinced otherwise. "No, if Emel were alive, I would have found him."

Galan took Adrina's hand. *Riders are still in the field.*

Father Jacob sighed. "A few, yes. They help clear the fields. Most have returned to the city to join in the celebrations. Emel is not among them."

A few, Galan said, sending disbelief along with the words, *I see hundreds.*

Father Jacob and Adrina followed Galan's gaze, a confused call going forth from the walls matched their surprise. That the large band of riders was Kingdom horse soldiers there was no doubt, but the rout of the enemy army had been completed before the day had even begun, and now the day was nearly over.

The jubilant soldiers' swords and lances glistened in the late afternoon sun. They did not race their mounts, instead they held them to a steady trot. The animals must have indeed been weary.

"Could it be?" Adrina asked.

Neither Galan nor Father Jacob had to respond to the question. At the fore of the group was a great black stallion. In Adrina's mind, there was no mistaking *Ebony Lightning,* Emel's beloved mount.

As the riders approached, their faces slowly became clear. Adrina knew that it was Emel who rode *Ebony.* What's more, Emel wasn't just at the fore of the pack, he was leading it and behind him were over three hundred Kingdom riders. Their shouts and cheers rose to the walls of Quashan' and trumpets returned their jubilant cries with increasing vigor. Those celebrating in the streets of Quashan', curious as to what the commotion was, came to the field, and soon thousands covered the near end of the field by the city's southern gate.

Father Jacob said, "His father would have indeed been proud

of him this day."

"Indeed," said a voice from behind them. At once Adrina recognized the voice of her brother. Prince Valam put his hand on Adrina's shoulder. "Captain Brodst will surely hear of it, for I will tell him myself on the day I see his son is promoted to Second Captain, Imtal Garrison."

"Second Captain?" Adrina asked surprised.

"Imtal Garrison is without two of her captains, and who better to fill the place than one who has proven himself worthy."

Adrina pointed a finger at Valam. "You knew where he'd been all along didn't you." Adrina wiped tears from her cheeks. "And you let me worry and fret—"

"I had a hunch, but I wasn't certain."

Before Adrina could reply, Emel reined in *Ebony* beside them. He was grinning ear to ear. He leapt from the saddle.

Adrina ran to him and hugged him fiercely. "I thought you dead. Where have you been?"

Emel laughed then said. "Making sure Jarom's army never returns to South Province without giving precious thought to the consequences. We chased them so far, and they ran so fast, I'd be surprised if they weren't still running."

"You will make a good captain, Emel," Valam said.

Adrina was still hugging Emel fiercely, and now Emel's face was a bit red. "Captain?" Emel asked.

"Captain," Adrina said, and she kissed him on the cheek.

Valam cleared his throat. Adrina stepped back, and Valam gripped Emel's shoulder. "Second Captain, Imtal Garrison. Captain Ghenson was a good man, and I know you will lead well in his stead."

A surge of celebrants and music came toward them. Dancers and musicians had made their way to the field from Quashan's many squares, stirring ever more excitement into the already boisterous crowd. Valam, Emel, Adrina, Galan and Father Jacob found they could do nothing other than join in.

Chapter Fourteen: Parting Ways

The celebrations continued for three days and nights. Every day since the destruction, artisans had been hard at work rebuilding the city. The Master Stonecutter had seen to the walls and his laborers and masons had them nearly as strong as they once had been. Already the city's smiths had the ironwork of the southern gate and portcullis restored. The city's woodworkers had started construction on dozens of new homes. And the fact that there was already a shortage of nails, timber and bricks, proved how hard everyone was working toward the city's restoration.

Vilmos was growing restless. It wasn't so much that he was tired of life in Quashan's keep, but he was unaccustomed to people paying so much attention to him. Serving girls made him uneasy by catering to his needs and treating him as he imagined visiting royalty must be treated. The room he and Xith shared held riches beyond anything he had ever dreamed of. The mattresses on the beds were made of hundreds, maybe thousands, of goose down feathers, as were the magnificently plush pillows. He had never imagined a bed could be made out of anything other than straw covered over or that a night's sleep could be so restful and refreshing.

The sheets were soft and silky smooth. Servants would draw him a bath each evening and he used scented soaps to wash with. He had been given fine clothes, a jeweled dagger to put in the scabbard at his belt, and handsomely crafted leather boots. No more ill-fitting boots.

Oddly, it was the absence of his old and worn boots that made him yearn for home. He wondered how Lillath and Vil fared, and hoped that no harm had come to them. He had told Xith of his vow that one day he would return home, and Xith had said that perhaps one day he could go home, but that day would be a long way off.

Vilmos looked at himself in the mirror again, made a face, and started to undress. Xith came into the room.

The shaman smiled, then said, "You look like a fine young man, come quickly. We cannot keep His Highness waiting."

Vilmos frowned, looked back into the mirror, then wordlessly followed Xith. He knew something special was planned for this evening, but what Xith hadn't told him.

They were descending the central stairs to the keep's great hall, when Vilmos asked, "Why all the secrecy? What is afoot?"

Xith stopped and faced Vilmos. "Enjoy yourself this evening. We will be leaving Quashan' in the morning. It is time to begin your education."

"Education?" Vilmos asked.

Xith didn't answer, instead he continued down the stairs.

Vilmos heard playful laughter in his mind and before he followed Xith, he glanced to the top of the stairs. Galan and Seth stood at the top of the landing. Galan wore a deep blue dress befitting a princess and Seth wore princely clothes matched to Galan's dress.

We will leave in the morning also, Galan said. Galan took Seth's hand as he offered it to her, and he led her down the stairs toward Vilmos. *Perhaps you will come with us to Imtal to speak to King Andrew.*

"I would like that," Vilmos said, "but I think Master Xith has other plans."

"Perhaps, perhaps not," Seth said. He spoke aloud. "But I fear we are nearly late and should hurry."

Vilmos smiled at Seth's spoken speech. Seth was working hard on his Kingdom accent.

Galan laughed again, and Vilmos heard its echo in his mind as she prodded him to chase after Xith.

Vilmos raced off to the keep's great hall. Seth and Galan followed.

***

Hundreds of guests were seated at the many tables encircling the hall's main table. At the head of the main table sat Prince Valam. Seated to his left were Chancellor Van'te, Keeper Martin, Father Jacob, Sergeant Danyel', Captain Adylton of Imtal and Captain Berre of Quashan'. Princess Adrina, the soon-to-be captain Emel, Vilmos, Xith, Seth and Galan were seated to his right. Vilmos was glad to be surrounded by a few friendly faces, for most of the others in the enormous hall were strangers to him.

Wonderful aromas rose from the kitchen at the northern end of the hall and, nearly out of sight, attendants waited to bring food to the tables. Vilmos glanced to the four empty seats around the table and wondered who they were reserved for, then bowed his head as Father Jacob began the before meal prayer.

Father Jacob concluded the prayer as he had the past seven evenings, by giving thanks to Great-Father for divine providence. Afterward, for a brief time, a discord of voices returned.

Vilmos looked about the hall.

Emel, to his left, said, "Still not used to it, are you?"

"To tell the truth, I would much rather eat somewhere more private."

"And miss all this?" asked Adrina. "Just wait till you see Imtal's hall."

Vilmos shrugged.

Emel whispered, "Me too."

Adrina asked Vilmos, "You will be coming with us to Imtal, won't you?" When Vilmos didn't answer immediately, Adrina glared, then added, "You must."

Vilmos turned expectant eyes to Xith.

"Alas," Xith said, "it is time we were on our way. Vilmos and I have much to do. He has an education to begin."

Adrina made a face.

Xith said, "Do not fret Princess. Seth and Galan will accompany you to Imtal, yet, I suspect that you have not seen Vilmos and I for the last time."

Vilmos was about to say something when Lord Valam cleared his throat, then stood. A sudden hush spread throughout as Valam's gaze swept around the hall.

"On the eve of the seventh day of the cleansing of our home, we celebrate." Valam raised a golden goblet. "We commemorate those who have fallen in the defense of their kingdom and honor those who helped achieve victory.

"It is unfortunate that this hall cannot hold each and every soldier presently residing in Quashan', for, down to the last man—" Adrina cleared her throat. "—and woman, they contributed to victory, and none more so than those of you seated here today. I, the citizens of Great Kingdom, and your king, thank you."

Valam raised the goblet above his head in salute, then drank from it until it was empty. A cheer went up, then everyone likewise honored the toast, Vilmos included, though he did not drink wine. Xith had warned him that he shouldn't and for good reason, because it was customary for each of the honored guests to likewise make a toast. Cheers followed every toast, empty wine bottles were hurled against the walls and attendants hurried about the room with new bottles.

When it came time for Vilmos to make a toast, he was so nervous that all he could manage to say was, "To Great Kingdom," and still the crowd cheered.

The last toast made, the cheers faded. Prince Valam stood. He raised his hand, commanding silence. "Several matters have come to my attention that demand addressing," he began. "First of all, the heroic deeds of those seated here—" Valam swept his hand around the central table. "—are largely unknown to all save a few. I wish to make public the knowledge of these deeds so that all may know and none will forget."

Keeper Q'yer was admitted to the hall. He carried a large tome and placed it before his prince.

❧ The Kingdoms & The Elves ❧

"Inscribed on these pages are the deeds of the twelve seated here before you as best as can be ascribed," read Valam aloud.

Valam looked to those around the table. "Please stand and be recognized as I read your name. Chancellor Van'te, once King Andrew's advisor who now serves Lord Valam. Keeper Martin, Head of Lore Keepers. Father Jacob, First Priest of Great-Father. Sergeant Danyel', Quashan' garrison. Captain Adylton, First Captain of Imtal garrison. Captain Berre, First Captain of Quashan' garrison. Princess Adrina, daughter of King Andrew. Sergeant Emel Brodstson, son of King's Captain Brodst. Brother Seth of the Red Order who are the Queen's Protectors. Brother Galan of the Red Order who are the Queen's Protectors. Master Xith, of Oread and wise shaman. And lastly, Vilmos, son of Vil, Counselor of Tabborrath Village."

Briefly Keeper Q'yer began recounting the deeds inscribed in the tome. Lastly he spoke of Princess Adrina, Galan and Vilmos' venture into Sever's camp and an audible murmur passed through the crowd. It was clear few knew of this event.

Valam said, "From this day hence, this tome shall be put in a glass case which will stand at the entrance of this keep so that all may look upon it and read the inscribed names, and those who stand before you shall be known as Quashan's protectors, heroes of the realm. Let the word go forth from this hall so that all may know."

Unrestrained cheers followed and it took Valam a few minutes to calm the enthusiasm.

"The next matter concerns my sister, Princess Adrina, who has decided to return to Imtal instead of staying the winter in our fair

South." Keeper Q'yer handed Valam a scroll. "This scroll contains a message to my father, King Andrew, that Adrina will conduct to Imtal. With my regrets that I must stay in the South, I send a request that the King grant Brother Seth and Brother Galan an audience that they are surely due."

Valam put his seal upon the scroll. Keeper Q'yer raised it for all to see. Then Valam said, "Now, I think it is about time we eat!"

A cheer went up and attendants hurried heavily laden plates to the tables. Keeper Q'yer sat at an empty place, and they were about to start eating when a page entered the hall. Valam took the roll of parchment the boy held. After reading the message, Valam whispered something to the page then the boy hurried off.

With his eyes, Vilmos followed the departing page until the boy disappeared into an adjacent corridor. A few seconds later, the page returned. Behind him were three men. One was a burly man dressed in a captain's uniform. The other two by their attire and poise seemed to be nobility, but their hair was fair and not dark as Adrina's or Valam's.

Vilmos turned back to regard Valam. Valam was grinning.

"One last thing," Valam said. "Please welcome, King's Captain Brodst and the guests he brings from Klaive. The Baron of Klaive, and his son, Rudden, conveyed a supply caravan of lumber from their hardwood forests and metal for nails from their mines to Quashan'."

Adrina, who was apparently shocked, seemed about to try to slip under the table.

"Greetings My Lord Valam," said the Baron of Klaive and his son.

"Please join us," Valam said. He clapped his hands and attendants rushed forward to seat the newcomers.

Rudden was seated directly across from Adrina, and Vilmos was now positive that she would at any moment slip under the table. Then she seemed to notice Emel, as Vilmos did just then. Emel was clearly jealous of the tall, good-looking southerner. Emel also seemed about ready to pull the arms off the high-backed chair he sat in.

Adrina's pout relaxed, faded, then she burst into laughter. Valam was quick to join in, as did most everyone else around the table, even Rudden who seemed a good sport.

"Let us eat!" Valam said.

And the meal began.

***

To Vilmos, it seemed Xith was disappointed or concerned, and certainly the shaman's thoughts were elsewhere at the moment. He stood in front of the chamber mirror and regarded his stomach. He smiled a boyish smile and whispered to himself, "Imagine me, a hero of the realm."

His mind still spun with the wonder of the hall. So much had happened. He had never seen so much splendor, never eaten so much food and never drank so much. His belly felt as if it were about to burst. This evening's events had certainly lived up to his expectations and would be something he wouldn't soon forget.

Still, he felt uncomfortable in the finery he wore. In the reflection of the mirror, Vilmos saw Xith changing into his customary robe. His eyes darted to a neatly folded pile of clothes. He picked them up and laid them out on the bed. He found that the chambermaid had darned his socks, patched the knees on his pants, and mended his shirt just as she had promised.

Without a second thought, Vilmos changed into his old clothes, and, while they weren't silk, they felt just as good. He turned back to face the mirror and found Xith standing in front of it. Xith was grinning.

"You look a fine young man," Xith said. "Those are clothes befitting one who is about to begin an education."

"I'm not sure I'm ready," Vilmos said.

Xith looked Vilmos up and down. "You are right, you aren't ready."

Vilmos frowned and a flood of disappointment swept over him.

Xith maintained his grin. "First I must—" Someone knocked on the door. Xith went over and opened it. Vilmos heard him say, "Your Highness, please come in."

Prince Valam stepped into the room. "I trust I am not disturbing you?"

Xith glanced to Vilmos then said, "Certainly not. Please come in."

"Adrina told me you planned to leave early tomorrow, so I slipped out of the hall for a moment to give you this." Valam handed Xith a rolled parchment. "It is something Father Jacob, Keeper Martin and I discussed at length—a writ, signed and closed with my seal. It is not as good as changing the King's law regarding magic, but I think it a close substitute. It guarantees safe passage for you and Vilmos through Great Kingdom and proclaims you lawful magicians."

The prince looked directly at Vilmos for a moment, then back to Xith. "I truly wish you would reconsider undertaking the journey to Imtal. I would rest easier knowing you were with Princess Adrina and the others as they return north. You would then be able to talk to my father, for only the King can change a law. But you would have my backing and that of Father Jacob and Keeper Martin."

Xith took the writ. "You are most gracious. This is much more than I had expected, and it is a first step. Yet centuries of superstition and fear cannot be erased with the wave of a hand. Let us not forget the reason magic is forbidden in the first place. Perhaps the day will come when the magus may again walk free and without fear. That day is not today nor tomorrow, but tomorrow's tomorrow."

Prince Valam's face lit up with mirth. "Father Jacob said you would say something like that, but I had to try… I will let you two get back to whatever it was you were doing before I arrived."

"Thank you, Your Highness," Xith said and he closed the door behind the prince.

When Xith turned back to Vilmos, some of the concern that had been in his eyes earlier had lifted. Vilmos started to say something, Xith hushed him and just then Xith revealed what he had been hiding behind the mirror. It was the staff Xith had been whittling, what seemed to Vilmos forever ago.

Xith asked, "Do you remember when I first showed you this?"

Vilmos knew all right, it had been the night before he and Xith entered Vangar Forest for the first time.

"Well, I have finally finished it and you have proven yourself worthy. What I was going to say earlier was that, first I must give you this before you are ready to begin. The staff is an extension of you."

Vilmos reached out for the staff, Xith pulled it back.

"Take it," Xith said, "and you will set your feet irreversibly upon the path to becoming the first Human Magus in five hundred years. What you have learned so far are simple cantrips to a true Mage. But be warned, you, Vilmos, are different. Just as I did not know if your dreams were truly gone, I do not know where the end of this path will take us."

Vilmos' heart was racing. His eyes were wide. He reached out and took the staff from Xith. Never had he been so sure of anything as he was right then when he touched the strange soft wood. His place was with Xith and wherever the path took him, he would follow.

Xith crossed to his bed and laid down on it. "Tomorrow will be a long day, there is so much we have to do."

Vilmos faced the mirror, grinned, then turned back to Xith. He asked, "Is Imtal truly as grand as Princess Adrina claims?"

Xith smiled, but didn't reply.

The story continues with:
The Kingdoms & The Elves of the Reaches
Book 3

About the Author

Robert Stanek is the author of many previously published books, including several bestsellers. Currently, he lives in the Pacific Northwest with his wife and children. Robert is proud to have served in the Persian Gulf War as a combat crewmember on an electronic warfare aircraft. During the war, he flew numerous combat and combat support missions, logging over two hundred combat flight hours.

His distinguished accomplishments during the Persian Gulf War earned him nine medals, including the United States of America's highest flying honor, the Air Force Distinguished Flying Cross. His career total was 17 medals in only 11 years of military service, making him one of the most highly decorated veterans of the Persian Gulf War.

Overwhelmingly, readers agree that Robert's books are among the best they've ever read. His books have very vocal supporters who aren't afraid to voice their opinion, and they frequently do so in online communities and lists, such as at Amazon.com, where you'll find that his books are consistently listed at the top of their class. Strong reader support has led to strong sales. The worldwide in print total for his books is quickly approaching 2 million.

About Reagent Press

Reagent Press is a small press that publishes both fiction and non-fiction titles. Current fiction titles include *Keeper Martin's Tale* and *Elf Queen's Quest* from the Ruin Mist Chronicles, *The Kingdoms & The Elves of the Reaches Book I* and *Book II* from Keeper Martin's Tales, and *The Elf Queen & The King Book I* and *Book II* from Ruin Mist Tales. Current non-fiction titles include: *Effective Writing for Business, College & Life*, *Essential Windows 2000 Commands Reference*, and *Essential Windows XP Commands Reference*.

Thank you for your continued support! Without the help of you, the reader, we will not be able to produce future works. If you liked this book, please tell your friends!

Ruin Mist Heroes, Legends & Beyond

Just about everyone that has read about Ruin Mist has wondered about the back story, where it all began, how the story all fits together, and now you can find answers in *Ruin Mist Heroes, Legends & Beyond*, a companion volume to the top-selling Ruin Mist books. *Ruin Mist Heroes, Legends & Beyond* allows you to learn about the dark elves of Under-Earth, common trades in the kingdoms, and beasts that go bump in the night. You can read the complete rules for King's Mate: the game, explore dozens of maps detailing the known realms, learn about the author, and more. In short, this is one book you shouldn't be without.

The Kingdoms & the Elves of the Reaches 2

Adrina, Emel, Vilmos, Galan and Seth must survive the greatest challenge Great Kingdom has faced in hundreds of years: the dissolution of the Kingdom Alliance and the battle to save Quashan'. Survival in a changing world depends on their ability to adapt and if they fail, their world and everything they believe in will perish.

The Kingdoms & the Elves of the Reaches 3

Adrina, Emel, Vilmos, Galan and Seth face even greater challenges as their world is transformed. Vilmos, in his quest to become the first human magus in a thousand years, must control the darkness within him. Adrina must accept her place and work together with Emel to help the elves make their plea to Great Kingdom's council. What happens along the way will amaze you.

Ruin Mist Tales

The Elf Queen & the King

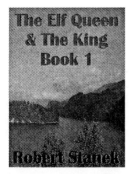

For every fantastic story you'll ever find there are often other stories that retell the adventures from different points of view—so why should it be any different in Ruin Mist? Join us now as we walk the dark path through the chronicles of Ruin Mist. Discover new secrets, new dangers, new visions and new realities!

The Elf Queen & the King 2

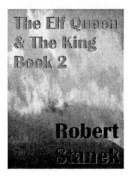

Dare to dream and slip away to Ruin Mist! What you find may surprise you... and journeys to Under-Earth are only the beginning. Can you survive the darkness?

Magic Lands

Following the village elder's advice, Ray leaves his home village, setting out for the place lost and deep where he will find a companion for his journey to the stone land and where he will discover that there is no easy path from childhood to manhood. "Beware lashing tail and gnashing teeth," the village elder warns him, "and if Old Bull doesn't get you, Mother Slither surely will."

Printed in the United States
907300003B